PICKLE

AND

PRICE

BY PIETER VAN RAVEN

The Great Man's Secret
Harpoon Island
Pickle and Price

PICKLE
AND
PRICE

PIETER
VAN RAVEN

CHARLES SCRIBNER'S SONS
NEW YORK

Charles Scribner's Sons Books for Young Readers
Macmillan Publishing Company
866 Third Avenue, New York, New York 10022
Collier Macmillan Canada, Inc.

First Edition   10 9 8 7 6 5 4 3 2 1
Printed in the United States of America

Library of Congress Cataloging-in-Publication Data
Van Raven, Pieter, date.
Pickle and Price / Pieter van Raven.—1st ed.   p.   cm.
Summary: Tired of living with an abusive father and an unloving mother who supervise a rural prison farm, thirteen-year-old Pickle and the released black convict he has befriended travel all the way across America in search of adventure, freedom, and a life free of discrimination.
[1. Runaways—Fiction.   2. Afro-Americans—Fiction.
3. Prejudices—Fiction.]   I. Title.
PZ7.V347Pi 1990 [Fic]—dc20   89–10846 CIP AC
ISBN 0–684–19162–8

For Henry De León

‖1‖

From the edge of the cornfield, Pickle could see the tall thin figure of Price bent over his hoe far down the row of seedlings. He ran toward him, careful not to tramp on the tender stalks rising out of the small hills of dirt.

Price looked up and leaned forward on the handle of his hoe. A sudden April breeze across the back of his sweaty denim shirt made him shiver. "Pickle," he asked, as the boy came near, "why aren't you in school? You skip out again?"

"Not this time," the boy shouted. "That's what I came to tell you. No more school this year."

"Have they closed the school? They passed a new law in this state that says a boy doesn't have to go to school after Easter? They have funny laws in this state, Pickle, but I never heard of that one."

"It's not that, Price. They still got school, right up through June like before, I reckon, but I ain't got no school. No more this year, anyways."

"You still haven't told me how come."

"I was expelled. Right there in class. The principal came in and took me to his office. He didn't ask the teacher if he could have me or nothing. He sat me down and told me I could go home, they'd start over with me next year. He gave me a letter for my ma telling her how come."

"She and your pa are going to thrash your bottom, Pickle. What did your ma say?"

"She ain't home. She's over to Aunt Vinnie's. There ain't nothing for her to do in the house when Pa and Myrna and me is gone. You seen Pa?"

"He took a gang in the bus over to the other field."

"Who's watching you, Price?"

"Nobody's watching me. You think I'm going to run away a week before they turn me loose? There's nobody that crazy."

The boy kicked a clump of red clay with his boot. "How long you been here, Price?"

"You know how long I've been here, Pickle. Damn near two years. Two years on the work farm, the judge said, and the two years is up in six days." Price looked at his watch. "Four hours less than six days at this very minute."

"How come you didn't get time off?"

"I didn't ask and they didn't offer. I don't have a law-yer to keep track of things for me. All of us on the farm do our time. Your pa says two years is two years, unless he says you don't behave; then it's six months more than two years."

Pickle had heard his father say often enough, "I ain't giving them boys time off. They serve their time."

Pa was mean, but fair, men on the gang told him. "Nobody runs off from your pa," they said. "They might end up at Old Man Weaver's over in Johnson County. That man likes to keep you forever."

Farm work wasn't all that hard, Pickle knew for a fact.

Last summer when he turned twelve, Pa sent him out to the fields right alongside the men. "I started when I was twelve," Pa had said. "You learn now what it's like on a prison farm, and you won't be wanting to come back on your own."

"What do you reckon Pa will do when he finds out?" he asked Price.

"He'll take the strap to you. I've seen him take it to some of the boys out in back of the washhouse when they were acting up. He's not supposed to, but he does. What did they expel you for, anyway?"

"'*Dis*-ruption,' the principal said. The other kids couldn't get on with their work because I was cutting up in class. That's what he said, '*dis*-ruption.'"

"I reckon your pa will take the strap to you every night until he forgets about it, Pickle. Just like he's going to take it to me if I don't finish my rows. Your pa's a hard man. He says he's fair, but I say he's hard."

Pickle walked toward the farmhouse. He could see the De Soto parked in the backyard. Ma and Myrna were home. He turned to study the sun hanging low over the pines at the far end of the field. He figured his father would be home pretty soon, too.

He wished Pa had stayed with the war and never come home. Aunt Vinnie looked after them pretty good while Pa was gone. She and Pickle got along better than Pickle and his mother, who didn't pay much attention to him except to scream at him not to make Myrna cry. Pickle didn't remember much of his father before he went off, mostly the soldier suit and how Pa threw Myrna up in the air, which made Ma holler, and caught her at the last minute coming down.

But Pa did come home, meaner than ever, Aunt Vinnie said. "Those Germans made your father as mean as they were, Pickle. I can say that of my very own brother, ain't that awful?"

Pa got the job running the county work farm. "Because you're so mean, Vernon," Aunt Vinnie told him to his face, "not because you're qualified or nothing." They packed up and they moved over to the farmhouse. Myrna was too big to throw up in the air, so Pa took to holding her on his lap. Pickle was big enough for a good licking every time he got out of line. Myrna was ten now and still sitting on Pa's lap after supper; Pickle was thirteen close to fourteen and still getting whipped regular.

If it wasn't for school, Pickle thought, things might be a lot different. Pa didn't take the strap to him too much before he started having trouble at school. Just wait until he was sixteen, the boy told himself. He counted the years on his fingers: just about two more years. He'd go into Lutherville and get a job driving trucks, like Uncle Marsh. He already drove the old Dodge truck around the farm, picking up the baskets of produce. Pickle counted on his fingers again. He'd be in the fifth or sixth grade by then, depending on how long he had to stay back in the fourth grade. Sixth grade was all the education he needed. Some of the men at the camp told him they never got farther than the third grade. A couple of them hadn't even gone to school at all.

A crow now settled down between the rows of corn. He pulled up a stalk, snapped off the kernel still on the plant, and strutted to the next stalk. Pickle bent down to pick up a hard clod of dirt. He tossed it in the air and let it fall to the ground. Let the old crow have the corn, he thought. It ain't none of my business.

As soon as he pulled open the screen door to the kitchen, Ma was on her feet, shaking the letter from the principal under his nose. "It's all over the school," she screamed, spit flying into Pickle's face. "Myrna heard it in her fifth-grade classroom. The kids were teasing her the rest of the day about her moron brother and made her cry. Ain't it bad enough to have her pass you at school, but you got to ruin her life, too? I'd whip you myself, but I reckon I'll wait for your pa to do it. He'll give it to you this time. And you ain't getting no supper tonight, do you hear?"

Pickle heard. He went out the front door and sat down next to Tick on the porch swing. He scratched under the hound's chin, and Tick licked his hand and went back to sleep. After a while the pickup rattled into the back yard. He heard the back door slam. His father came to the porch and spoke through the screen. "Come with me, boy."

Pickle couldn't see, but he knew Pa had the strap in his hand. It had been his grandfather's once. His father bragged it had been used on his backside until he was eighteen and had begun to act like a man. He reckoned he'd have to use it on Pickle until the day he died.

He followed Pa into the garage, which was full of broken machinery his father never got around to fixing. Pa had to take him out to the garage to get his whipping. Ma said she didn't want Myrna to grow up seeing her brother strapped in the kitchen. Ma used to bend him over a kitchen chair for a couple of licks with the switch, but Pa was different. He hurt, and he didn't stop until Pickle sniffled and then cried and finally howled. That was too much for Myrna. She'd cry, too, and run upstairs to her room.

"You ain't no better than a colored boy," Pa said as he doubled the strap to make it loose. "I'll have to learn you the same way."

When he finished, he told the boy, still bent over the tractor tire, "You be out here waiting tomorrow night, when I get home. I ain't going to fetch you. You be here. This time I'm going to learn you good."

|| 2 ||

His mother shook Pickle by the shoulder. "Your pa says you're to get out to the field and weed the corn with the convicts. There's some biscuits on the table. Put them in your pocket for lunch. And don't make no noise to wake Myrna up. I'm going back to my bed."

Pickle shut his eyes and rolled over, pulling his legs up to his stomach. He gasped with pain. His backside felt like it had been barbecued. He pulled himself to the edge of the bed and got to his feet. Cautiously he slipped his overalls up over one of Pa's old shirts Ma had laid out. He could not bend over to put on his socks. He shoved his feet bare into his work boots. Laces slapping on the steps, he went down to the kitchen.

Six of last night's biscuits lay on a cracked plate in the middle of the kitchen table. Pa had already drunk all the coffee in the pot. Pickle took the jug of buttermilk from the refrigerator and poured himself a glass. He drank it down with bits of dry biscuits. He pushed four biscuits into his pocket. He snatched his straw hat from the nail by the back door, grabbed his hoe, and hurried to the cornfield.

His father was driving the school bus down the dirt

road on the other side of the field. He stopped every ten rows or so to let one of the men out. When the bus had disappeared, Pickle lifted his head. He waved to Price, who was starting to work at the other end of the row.

When they came together toward the middle of the row, Pickle asked, "Who's out today?"

"Barnett. He doesn't even try to work us. All he does is find a patch of shade for himself and squat down with his gun across his knees. We could all walk to the state line before Barnett would find out."

"Pa says he's good for nothing."

"He's good enough for watching a work gang. It doesn't take any brains for that, just a mean disposition. Did your pa lick you?"

Pickle looked around. The other men were attending to their work. He unbuckled his overalls and lowered them to his knees. He dropped the tan army shorts Pa had brought home from the war and turned over to Pickle when he got big enough to wear them with a tuck in back.

Price whistled. "Man, he really gave it to you good. Did your ma put lard on it?"

"Nah. She gave me some Vaseline. It don't do no good. I'm going to catch it again tonight soon as Pa gets home."

"If he keeps beating you like that, he'll put you in the hospital, boy. How come your ma lets him do that to you?"

"She don't care as long as she's got Myrna. They don't care much what happens long as I stay out of trouble."

"Well, there's no trouble out here if you do your rows," Price said. "And I aim to keep on doing mine until next Tuesday morning. I'm getting my papers, and

I'm kissing this state good-bye forever. Until then this convict isn't causing anybody any trouble."

When Price got his release, Pickle wouldn't have any friends in the fields. The other men weren't about to have truck with the head man's boy. If they were talking when he brought around the pail, they'd stop until he moved on. The black men joked with him a little bit sometimes, because they had seen Price and him together, but the white guys took their dipperful and turned away.

He wondered if Price was going back to Detroit, that place up north where he had been going to high school. It didn't seem fair what happened to him. When he asked Pa about it once, all he said was that Price should have stayed up north where he belonged, they had enough of his kind down here already.

Price had come down to Lutherville with his ma to visit with her family. He and his cousin Clarence were driving out in the country in a car Clarence borrowed when the police came down the road in back. Clarence pulled over and ran off into the woods.

"Clarence hadn't borrowed that car." Price laughed. "He stole it. They carried me into town and put me in jail for an accessory. I said I was just hitching, but they didn't believe me. Clarence didn't bother to come bail me out. I reckon he was scared. There was no point in both of us being locked up. I took my two years. But I did want to finish school. I was thinking of going to the state university."

Price had already done a year in the reformatory when he was sixteen for stealing stuff from stores, he told Pickle. He made his mind up when he got out he wasn't going back. The work farm was better by a long shot than the reformatory. He told Pickle, "Those boys in the reformatory weren't just bad. They studied being bad."

If Price liked school the way he said he did, Pickle hoped he could finish. He was different from the rest of the men. They were sort of like Pickle, roughnecks and uneducated, most of them. The more he thought about it, he didn't see much difference between them and Pa. The only thing was they were in the camp and Pa was running it. Pickle wasn't itching to be like either one or the other. If only it wasn't for school. He and school didn't get along.

When the sun reached the top of the pines, the school bus came back to pick up the men waiting at the end of their rows. "I'll see you tomorrow, Pickle," Price said. "Maybe your pa will forget to whip you."

"He ain't going to forget. He told me to wait for him out in the garage. Soon as he gets you back to the bunkhouse, he'll be there all right."

There was no point in going inside. Ma was frying grits and sausage; he could smell it. Pickle wasn't all that hungry. He leaned against the garage door until he heard the noise of the pickup. Then he went inside and leaned over the tractor tire, head down on his folded arms.

The strap cut into his blistered bottom like a knife. Pickle clenched his teeth, his mind set on not crying out. After the fourth savage blow, he screamed—and screamed and screamed. His father stopped and stepped back. "Go inside," his father said. "Tell your ma I'm going over to the camp. Leave my supper on the table."

Pickle limped into the kitchen, each step sending a flash of pain through his butt and legs.

His mother pulled down Pickle's overalls and underwear. She took the kettle from the stove and filled a basin with warm water. He could smell the vinegar she mixed in with the water. "This is going to sting," she told him. "He had no call beating you like this." She pressed a warm cloth to his bottom.

"Myrna," she shouted, "Bring me down a pair of Pickle's underwear. Close your eyes when you come into the kitchen. I don't want you looking at your brother naked."

When she finished, Ma helped Pickle into the clean underwear. "Go up to bed now, 'less you want some supper. I'll tell your pa you can't go to no field tomorrow. Try to sleep on your stomach, Pickle."

After she took Myrna to the school bus stop the next morning, Ma stuck her head in the door. "I'm going over to Aunt Vinnie's for a while. I reckon you'll be all right. There's sausage on the table if you have a mind to it." In a softer voice, she said, "I don't hold with what your pa done, Pickle. Whipping a boy is one thing, hurting him like that is another thing. But if anyone ever had a call to take a strap to a boy, we surely do. Your pa says he has to beat some sense into you, and that's what he's going to do." With that warning, his mother drove off to Aunt Vinnie's.

When he was sure Ma was well down the road, Pickle crawled out of bed. His skin was stiff and hot to the touch. He shivered with a chill. He supposed he had a touch of fever. He had been hot and cold most of the night.

Pickle shuffled to the stairs. He went down a step at a time. At the bottom he realized he was talking to himself. "I ain't going to take it no more," he was saying. "I ain't no mule." He stood beside the table eating a cold sausage patty.

"No!" he said, out loud now. "That's it. No more whipping. I'll tell him to his face. 'You ain't going to beat me no more. I ain't no convict. I won't let you.'"

Pickle remembered he had said something like that once when Pa went to get his strap. Pa had turned around and slapped his face and darkened his eye and took the strap to him afterward.

He inched his way up the steps and into Ma and Pa's room. He reached up into the far corner of their closet shelf. He felt the holster and took it down. He carried it to the window. He drew the pistol from the holster. It was the service revolver Pa had in the war when he was a military policeman. At the other end of the closet shelf he kept his helmet with an *M* and a *P* on the front.

Pickle broke the gun open the way he had seen his father do it. He spun the cylinder. The pistol smelled of oil Pa put on it to keep the rust off. He pushed it back into the holster and returned it to the shelf. It would be there when he needed it, he told himself.

The bullets were in the top drawer of the bureau under Pa's red bandanna handkerchiefs. Pickle dumped them out of the little box onto the unmade bed. He counted them, eleven in all. They didn't look like much resting there in his hand, but he had heard Pa say one of them would stop an elephant. Pa was big and tough himself, but he wasn't no elephant. Pickle lined the bullets up in the box and put it back under the handkerchiefs.

Pa didn't bother with him the next couple of days. Pickle heard Ma tell him to leave the boy be or she'd call the doctor, and how was Pa going to tell the doctor Pickle got his butt cut up? Ma didn't say much to Pickle either. She brought him a plate of chicken one day, and on Sunday before she and Pa and Myrna went off to the church picnic she left a pitcher of lemonade in the refrigerator with some sandwiches.

It was on Sunday in the empty house that the idea began to form in Pickle's head. The fever had gone away, and his bottom stopped aching so much. He could move around pretty good. He went out to the yard to have a look at the Dodge. Pa always left the key. "This is the last place them boys will come to steal the car," he used to say.

Pickle turned the key. In the middle of the day the pickup started right off. On a damp morning it gave Pa a lot of trouble. Pickle got out and lifted the hood. He had seen one of the men work on it once when it wouldn't run. There was a wire loose. Pickle pulled the one he thought the convict had connected. The motor coughed and stopped. He attached the wire and closed the hood.

Tick was on the front porch swing, where he spent all his time except in the fall when Pa dragged him to the woods to hunt possum. Pickle gave Tick half his sandwich. He swung back and forth making his plans.

‖ 3 ‖

Ma was making coffee and cooking Pa's eggs early Monday morning when Pickle came down. He went straight on through the kitchen and out the back door.

"Don't you want no breakfast?" Ma called after him.

Pickle didn't answer. He took his hoe and cut across the yard. Ma yelled after him to wait. She came out in her housedress and felt slippers, her hair in curlers.

"Here," she said, shoving a paper bag at him. "I brought some doughnuts home from the picnic for Myrna's lunch, but they got hard and she won't take them." She stopped for a minute. "Your pa's going to whip you tonight. Maybe not so hard, but he's going to do it. He says he told you he was going to and he's going to. I don't hold with that, but there ain't nothing I can do."

Pickle shrugged and headed for the field. By the time the bus dropped the men off, Pickle had almost finished with his first row. The seedlings were coming up fast, and the weeds just as fast. Pickle remembered the heat last summer as soon as the corn got shoulder high and cut out the breeze. This year it would be different. He was going to see to that.

"You did my row for me, Pickle, did you?" Price

asked. "Tomorrow you are going to do yours *and* mine, I bet. Your pa's going to keep you out of trouble."

"Maybe," Pickle answered. He offered Price one of the picnic doughnuts.

Price bit into it. "They're hard, man. Where'd you get these?"

"Ma gave them to me. Myrna didn't want them."

"I reckon the crows won't either," Price said, "so I better eat it myself. Your pa said you were to carry water today between times."

"Where'd they put the drum?"

"Under the tree, down at the corner. Barnett, he's looking after it for you. I'm going to work, Pickle. Your pa's not getting any excuse today to keep me here."

There wasn't any sense in telling Price his plans, Pickle decided. He might try to talk him out of them. He bit off half a doughnut and threw the other half on the ground for the crows.

In the middle of the morning, Pickle went down to the corner of the field. Barnett was sitting with his back against the pine tree, his hat down over his eyes. He jumped when Pickle lowered the tin bucket into the oil drum.

"It's only you, Pickle. You gave me a start. I thought maybe it was one of the boys creeping after me with a razor." Barnett patted the stock of his shotgun. "Don't I wish," he said. "Don't I wish one of them would make a move."

"It ain't so hot today," Pickle said. "How many times ought I to go round?"

"Many as you want, Pickle. Carrying water is better than hoeing wet clay. Your pa going to beat you tonight?"

"I guess."

"He said he was going to. You're pretty big to be getting whipped, don't it seem to you?"

The boy did not reply. He walked back down the road with the bucket, water slopping over the top into his boots.

"What time you leaving tomorrow, Price?" he asked his friend.

"Ten o'clock, that's checkout time. It gives you two hours to walk to town and catch the Trailways. I won't have time to go looking for Cousin Clarence to let him know how I feel."

"Maybe you can catch a ride to town," Pickle said.

Price looked at him hard. "Do you suppose somebody's going to come by and give a black boy a ride when he's walking down the road from the work camp? No, sir, I'm on my own. I can walk five miles before noon easy. You want to come along with me, Pickle?" he teased. "Your pa's going to pay me just about enough for two tickets to Detroit."

"Maybe," Pickle said. "Maybe I just will. I'll tell you later."

The next time around with the bucket, Price was eating lunch with the black boys. He didn't have time for Pickle. They drank their water and went on laughing about what Price was going to do when he got to Detroit City.

Pa came down the road in the Dodge pickup. "Get in," he ordered.

Pickle held up the bucket to ask what to do with that.

Pa stuck his head out the window "LeRoy," he shouted, "You take care of the water, hear?" And to Pickle, "Get in, I said."

Pickle got in. He sat as close to the door as he could

and put his face into the breeze. Pa drove to the house. "Get out. You clean out the garage this afternoon. The county's buying me a new truck."

Pickle's heart sank. He had told himself he'd never speak to his father, but he had to know about the truck. "What kind is it? When you getting it?" he asked.

"I told them a Chevy. That's what I had in the war. Next week, they said in town."

"The tractor won't start. We'll have to push it out."

"We'll do that tonight after the whipping. You get everything else out. Put it around in back."

Pa gave him five whacks, more for appearance's sake than to hurt him. Still, they made Pickle's sensitive bottom smart. Pa didn't say anything, just gave him his five licks and motioned for him to help push the old John Deere out of the garage to make room for the new pickup.

Pickle woke at the first light. His mind snapped to attention. He listened. Pa was snoring so hard the house shook. In the hallway he paused. Myrna was trying to swallow her thumb. That meant she wasn't resting easy. He crept down the stairs, passing over the one that creaked no matter where you stepped on it. There was the smell of fried sausage in the kitchen that was always there except in the winter when the wood stove dried up all the smells.

The hood of the Dodge was drenched with dew. He lifted it up carefully. The rusty metal creaked. Pickle paused. Tick came around from the front porch to see what was going on. He rubbed against Pickle's leg.

When the hood was high enough, Pickle cocked it open with a chunk of firewood. He felt inside for the wire. He pulled it loose. He eased the hood back down. Pa would blame the damp the way he always did when the Dodge wouldn't start up. He'd have to take the De Soto and carry Myrna to the bus stop and drop Ma off at Vinnie's if she was going there.

Pickle slipped back into his room. Ma would be up soon to get Pa's breakfast and pack Myrna's lunch. He put the pillow over his head and held his breath as long as he could. Then again. He put his hand to his forehead. It felt a little hotter. He pulled the pillow tight and held his breath some more.

"What's the matter with you, Pickle?" his mother said. She slid her hand under the pillow to feel his head. "You got a fever? You don't feel hot."

"All night I was hot and my head hurt," Pickle whispered.

"I reckon it was too much sun yesterday being out in the field after three days in bed. You stay here today. It'll go away. I'll tell your pa."

She came back with four aspirin and a glass of water. She told him to take two right away and the other two around noon. There was still some lemonade in the refrigerator, and she'd make an extra sandwich. "I got to go to Vinnie's today. I promised I'd help her on the quilt for the church bazaar. You'll be all right here."

His father stuck his head in on his way downstairs. "Don't think you're going to get out of a licking being in bed. I'll catch you tomorrow."

"Louella," Pickle heard him shout. "Hurry up. I need the De Soto." He started the De Soto and let it run to dry off the windows. Exhaust floated up to Pickle's window. It smelled good in the damp air. He took the pillow off his head and leaned back, hands behind his head. He smiled. So far, so good.

At seven-thirty the De Soto rolled down the lane to get Myrna to the bus stop. The school bus came at twenty of. Sometimes Pickle took the bus when Ma made him get in the car with Myrna. Mostly he got out of the house long before she thought of leaving and walked to school. It took about an hour unless he dawdled, which he must of done most of the time, because he had a whole line of late marks after his name.

Not anymore, he thought. I ain't going to have to be late *or* early. When he estimated it was eight-thirty and neither Ma or Pa was likely to come back for something they might of forgot, Pickle climbed out of bed. He took the army kit bag from Ma's closet. There was a nightgown and some slippers and extra hair curlers inside for when Ma took Myrna to spend the night at Aunt Vinnie's, to get away from the farm for a day or two, she said. He shook them out on the bed.

From his bureau he took two pairs of striped overalls and a pair of regular pants, all the shirts and underwear he had, and some socks. The only shoes that fit were the boots he wore every day. He would buy some later.

He went back into his parents' room. He reached up on the shelf for the holster. He took out the gun. He put six bullets from the box in the cylinder. He weighed the gun in the palm of his hand, then closed his fist around it. He pointed out the window at the John Deere. "Pow," he said softly. He made sure the safety was on. He shoved the gun back in the holster and snapped the flap down. He slipped it into the bottom of the kit bag. "I'm not coming back," he muttered. "Sure as shootin',

I'm not coming back." He laughed at his joke. "There's no way I'm coming back."

Pickle poured the last of Myrna's Rice Krispies into a bowl. He leaned back in his kitchen chair, feet on the table, and studied the kitchen clock. Price must be getting out free pretty soon. He'd give him a little more time. He drank the last of the cold coffee from Pa's cup, the heavy china cup with a duck on it that Pa had said belonged to his father. He wouldn't let no one else so much as touch it. Pickle held it high and let it drop. It bounced on the linoleum and rolled unbroken under the table. He bent to pick it up. Shoot, it wasn't the cup's fault what happened. He washed it under the tap and dried it off.

He pushed a chair over to the china shelf. Up in back of the company china Ma never used because she said it was too good for any company *they* had, she kept her savings in a mason jar. Pickle dumped it out on the table. He wasn't sure how much was in the jar. More than he would ever need. He would have to buy gas. That was for sure. He wondered how much things like gas and bread and a pair of shoes cost. Ma hadn't taken him to the store with her much. He took two bills with a twenty in the corners and a handful of change. That ought to be enough. He tucked the jar back up on the top shelf.

The big hand on the clock was pushing up toward the top. That meant it was almost ten o'clock, he told himself proudly. He took the plate of cold sausage from the refrigerator and carried it out to the front porch for Tick. He was about to put the plate down when he thought there was no need to get Ma mad with Tick, too. He dumped the sausage on the porch and put the empty plate back in the refrigerator.

Pickle guessed it was time to go. He tucked the kit bag under his arm like his father did instead of carrying it by the straps and went out to the Dodge. He connected the wire. He got inside and pushed the squeaky old starter. The motor turned over, once, twice, and started to purr like a Cadillac. Pickle shoved it into first and headed out of the yard.

4

Price was striding along the road on the left ahead of him. He was carrying a paper bag the men got when they were turned loose. Pa took money out of their pay for the work farm clothes, and they got to keep the clothes.

There was nothing coming on the road either way. Pickle eased the Dodge across the road and came up real slow behind Price who didn't pay any attention. Pickle blew the horn. The blast made Price jump into the ditch.

Pickle rolled the window down. "I reckon that made you jump, Price. Get on in."

Price climbed up the bank. "What did you do that for, Pickle? You could have just pulled up and said good-bye."

"I came by to give you a ride to Detroit City. Get on in."

"I don't have time to joke with you, Pickle. The Trailways leaves at noon. They won't be holding the bus for a black man to show up. When your pa finds out you're driving his truck on the county road, he'll whip your butt for another week. Aren't you too young to have a driver's license?"

"You don't need a license in this state, long as you can

drive. It's the only state in the union like that, Pa said. I been driving the pickup for years. Come on, get in."

Price started to move on down the road. "You take care, Pickle," he called back. "It's been nice knowing you. Get on home before you come up with more trouble than you're looking for."

Pickle drove the truck up in front of Price. He stopped, blocking his way. He got out. "Durn it, Price. I drove this truck out here to give you a ride home. I packed a bag and everything and borrowed some of Ma's money without her knowing it. I ain't going back. I go back now, and Pa will most likely kill me, or worse." He figured Price didn't need to know about the gun just yet.

Price looked at him in surprise. "You stole your pa's truck?"

"Yeah."

"And your ma's money?"

"Yeah."

"You know what that makes you, Pickle?"

"Yeah, a convict like you."

"No, it makes you a fool. Not a convict like me. I gave up being a convict. I've decided to finish school and go to state university like I planned and be a teacher or something. Don't stand there looking dumb, Pickle. You're already in enough trouble. Turn that pickup around and drive it back to the farm and don't break the speed laws on the way."

Price put out his hand. "It was good of you to think of me. I can find my way to town. I'll be seeing you up in Detroit when you have your own rig and come through town."

"I'll shake hands, Price, because we're friends. But we're going together. I can't take the strappings no more. I'm getting to be a man. Pa ain't got no right to beat me the rest of my life. I figure I'll see the country and come back in a couple of years. Maybe they'll be glad to see me then."

A new Studebaker with an airplane nose came down the road from town. It pulled over to the other side. Dr. Yancey leaned out the window. "You all right, Pickle? That truck died on you, did she? Took a long time. I'll drive you on back home."

"Nah, thanks, Dr. Yancey. I reckon we can get her started again. We always do. I was taking this boy into town to catch the bus."

Dr. Yancey started his car. "I'll see you, Pickle."

Price looked at his watch. "I got to get moving, or I'll miss my bus."

"Get in. I'll drive you to the depot."

"The last time I got in a stolen car they called me an accessory and put me in the work farm. No, thank you, Pickle. I'll just hurry along." Price stepped past the truck and trotted down the side of the road.

Pickle ran after him to grab his arm. "Ain't nobody going to arrest you. Me either. You know that. They know who my pa is around here. I'll ride you to the depot."

Price looked down at Pickle. He shook his head sadly. "If that's what you want, Pickle, that's what you get. Then you drive straight back home. Don't tell your pa you gave me a ride anywhere. There's bound to be a law in this state that says I'm not supposed to ride in the county's truck."

He opened the door and climbed in. He put his paper bag in the middle, on top of the kit bag. The boy crossed over to the right and headed for Lutherville at a steady thirty miles an hour.

"You were really going to leave, were you?" Price asked. "Got your clothes and everything?"

Pickle nodded. "No point in staying where you're not wanted. Lots of times Pa told me to get out if I didn't like it where I was. I'm getting out."

"You going to your aunt's? She's been good to you."

"Nah, maybe I'll go to California or Texas. I ain't made my mind up yet."

Price laughed. "You're not going anywhere. Do you know what it says on the side of this truck? Bedford County State Farm, that's what it says. By noontime the highway patrol and the sheriff will be out looking for this old Dodge, and it won't take them long to find it. It's not your pa's, you know. At first they're going to think one of the men—me, most likely, except I can't drive—stole the truck and took your ma's money, too. All I want is a ride to the depot before they start looking. No more trouble for me. You got that, Pickle?"

Price settled back. By now the heat shimmered over the tar road ahead. It was hot. Riding to town did beat walking. He wondered what was going to happen to Pickle. He was a nice kid. His pa had no business treating him so bad. At least he had a pa, for whatever that was worth. He rolled his shoulders. He felt strong and healthy. That was one thing two years of steady work had done for him. Made him into a man. He'd be all right now, once he got home to his mother.

They were coming into Lutherville through the black section. They passed a familiar white bungalow sitting on cinder blocks with a rundown garage in back and a couple of dead cars outside. Price straightened up and looked back. "Hey, that's Cousin Clarence's place. Do you reckon I ought to stop and give him a whipping?"

Tires squealing, Pickle turned the truck around in the middle of the road. He drove the Dodge through the side yard, past the dead cars, and into the garage between the junk.

‖ 5 ‖

Price kept his eye on the kitchen clock. He didn't have much time to get to the depot if he walked, and he was going to make sure he walked. Clarence was telling Pickle again and again how grateful he was to Price for not turning him in. He would have been sentenced to the work farm for at least five years. It was a white man's car he borrowed by mistake.

"You ain't going to tell on me, are you, boy? Not after all this time? I got a steady job now in the repair shop."

"Naw," Pickle said. "I ain't going home anyway."

"He's going home, Clarence. Pickle's just talking," Price broke in. "He's going home right now. And I'm going to the depot. How come you're not at work?"

"I took the day off," Clarence answered evasively. "I don't let them think they own me. Take the day off once in a while."

"Let's go, Pickle," Price ordered. "I let you bring me to town like you wanted. It's time to turn that truck around and head for home before the highway patrol takes after you. When your ma gets back from Chicago, Clarence, tell her I dropped by."

"She ain't coming back for a month. Not until my sister finds someone to look after the baby so's she can go back to work. Why don't you relax and spend some time sitting here on the porch?"

"Looking at wrecked cars? No, thank you. I'll be on my way. Come on, Pickle. I'll show you how to get back to the road out front, in case you can't find it."

Clarence came out to the garage. He studied the old Dodge. "That's a county truck, ain't it? Where'd you get that from? Your pa?"

"He stole it, like you stole that white man's Pontiac, only I'm not going to jail on account of what he did. He's taking it back."

"You go on up north, Price," Pickle answered. "I ain't going home. I'll wait here until dark with Clarence and take on off. They ain't going to find the truck in the garage here."

Clarence walked around the truck. He kicked the tires. He lifted the hood to study the motor. He slammed the doors. "That truck's in mighty fine condition, being as old as it is. Don't do nothing but run around the farm, I reckon. Must be one of the last ones they made before the war. Yes, sir, that's a good truck. If you was of a mind to keep on going, I could fix that pickup so's it'd run another ten—twelve years. Give it a coat of paint, too. That would help. Got some rust on it."

"What are you talking about, Clarence?" Price asked.

"If the boy has his mind set on going to California or wherever, I might as well help him. I owe you something for what you done for me. I'll pay the boy here back, instead. Nothing I can do for you up in Detroit. Look at it like this, Price. If I fix up the county farm truck for the head man's boy, you might say I'd be serving some time I owe the state, ain't that so?"

"Would you?" Pickle asked excitedly. "You'd fix it up for me?"

Price looked at his watch. He was going to miss the bus. There was no way he was going to get to the Trailways before noon. He wondered when the next bus came through.

Clarence answered his question. "You done missed it, Price, standing around here arguing. The next express bus up north comes through tomorrow noon, same as today. Go make yourself some coffee. The boy and I got to talk about this Dodge truck."

"That boy is on his own now. When they come around to get him, Clarence, you just be sure you're the accessory this time."

"They aren't coming around here to get nobody. Yes, sir, we'll fix it up so's they'll never know it. We'll give it a coat of paint first. I'll go over to the shop and get a spray gun. What do you think, Pickle? Dark blue ain't going to call attention to you. And I'll give you a set of new plates."

"Then Clarence is going to work on the rest of it," Pickle explained to Price in the kitchen. "Three days, he says, for two coats of paint and an overhaul, unless he needs some parts."

Price sipped his coffee. He wanted no part of what was going on. He'd be sure to be first in line for the bus tomorrow.

"You understand, Pickle, I have nothing to do with this. You are Clarence's responsibility, do you understand? What you and Clarence are doing is illegal, and you being your father's boy doesn't make it legal. Clarence, he's going to end up on the farm. I don't know what's going to happen to you, since strapping doesn't do any good. Your pa will think of something. Get it into your head, Pickle, you're fooling around with dynamite."

"Maybe," Pickle admitted, "but Clarence is right. No one's going to be looking for the truck out here. No, sir, not for one minute."

"Once you drive out of here, they're going to catch you, no matter what color Clarence takes it into his head to paint it. You go on out and help Clarence if you want to. I'm going to clean up this kitchen. Clarence hasn't washed a dish since his ma went off."

"Just don't push Cousin Price right away," Clarence advised Pickle. They were taping newspaper over the windows and the running board and the chrome parts. "We get started on this, and he'll come around tomorrow or the next day. It ain't no fun riding in the back of a Trailways bus when you can be riding in the front of a new Dodge pickup. Ma couldn't even get something to eat until she got to Chicago. Those bus stops is just for white people. Now, you take this steel wool and wherever you see any rust, you rub it down."

Price did not recognize the truck the next morning. Clarence had put it up on blocks and was underneath working on the pipes and muffler. Pickle was hard at work on the bumpers and trim with a can of aluminum paint. "When you going to be done?" Price called underneath to Clarence.

"Tomorrow night."

"You still going to California, Pickle?"

"Clarence showed me the map. He said I should go by way of Detroit in case you asked. It's out of the way, he says, but I don't mind none. I ain't in no hurry."

"How much money you got?"

Pickle pulled out his two bills and the change. "Here,

you count it. I ain't much good at counting money. They ain't got to money in the fourth grade."

Price counted forty-three dollars and sixty cents. "How much is gasoline?" he hollered to Clarence.

"It all depends. Say thirty cents a gallon."

"And how many miles does this truck get to a gallon of gas?"

"After I get done tuning it up, maybe fifteen out on the highway. They put a lot of weight in these trucks. They use up gas like it was water. I can't do nothing about that."

Price took the map off the seat. He sat down on a cinder block and spread it across his knees. He calculated the distance and multiplied. "Well, you got plenty of money for gas, if you were to go that way."

Price realized he wasn't about to persuade Pickle to go home, now that Clarence had made him a new truck. He figured he'd be tired of driving by the time he reached Detroit. Pickle would be happy to take the bus back to Lutherville. He could tell his Pa the truck was stolen or something. The boy *looked* sixteen. If he didn't speed, he wasn't going to get stopped.

What was he thinking? What was he planning to do? He was thinking trouble, that's what he was doing. But the boy needed help. There was no telling what might happen to him on the road to California. He'd never been off the farm in his life except to go to school. What the hell, Price thought. There wasn't going to be any trouble; he'd see to that.

"How come they call you Pickle?" Price asked. "Is it some kind of a nickname?" He was staring hard down the road in the glare of the pickup's headlights. The road looked different at night, mysterious off on the sides beyond the lights. You could smell the fields in the soft night air. Clarence was right. It did beat riding the Trailways.

"Naw, it's my real name, only it ain't ought to be pronounced Pickle. That's just what they call me. My full name is John Pick*el* Sherburn. Ma says those are two fine southern names. Her folks are the Pick*els*. Colonel Pickel was in the Civil War. He was killed up north. The Sherburns were in the war, too, Pa said; after that, the Sherburns and Pickels didn't amount to much. What's your name, Price?"

"I'm just my mama's boy, Price Douglas. Mama never told me what the Price was for, except that it wasn't for my father."

"Where's your pa at? Is he dead?"

"Nobody knows where he's at. Or, if they know they haven't told me. My sister, she doesn't know either."

"You got a sister, too, like me?"

"Not like you exactly. Ruth, she's older than me. She and her husband live down the street from Mama. They got two girls. George, he works at the GM plant. They make cars. George never said what kind he makes."

"Maybe he made this old Dodge. He made a good one if he did."

"GM doesn't make Dodges. They make Chevys and Cadillacs and I don't know what else, Buicks maybe."

That reminded Pickle that Pa was getting a new pickup next week. He wouldn't care so much about losing the Dodge when he had a new Chevy pickup that would start every morning. Pickle didn't feel much of anything about running away from home. Maybe a little bit sad about Ma. But she had Myrna, and Myrna was all she ever wanted anyway. Myrna with her hair bows, Myrna with her shiny patent leather shoes just like the ones Becky Church had in the moving pictures, Myrna with her china dolls all lined up at the foot of her bed. Maybe he should have busted them up before he left. That would teach Myrna not to be carrying home tales on him from school.

"Slow down, Pickle. I do believe, yes, sir, it is the state line. You are now in the act of leaving the state where you were born and brought up. Bid it good-bye and pray they don't keep after you."

"I don't reckon they will. They didn't want me, and Pa's getting a new truck," Pickle answered.

Price rested his chin on the open window. He looked at the bramble fence along the edge of the shadows. Every once in a while they passed a farmhouse or a cabin with a light in the window. There was a magic in the darkness that started at the bramble fence and kept on going all the way to China. You couldn't only see it, you could smell it and taste it if you opened your mouth and let the air rush in. It wasn't ever like that on Lansing Avenue. The streetlights came in through the shades, and the cars and buses rolled by until it was almost dawn. And the kids were always making some kind of noise.

The reformatory was out on the edge of the city, and there were lights everywhere: lights in the corridors, lights in the yard, flashlights poking into your room any old time of night to see if you were still there. No corner to hide in there. Here the darkness was a blanket you could hide under forever.

Price had the urge to stop before it changed. "Pickle," he asked, "you going to drive all night?"

"I don't know. I ain't tired yet. I never drove much at night before. Anyway, where we going to spend the night? I don't rightly know where we're going. You said you was reading the map for me."

"Well, I can't read it in the dark, can I? Don't you suppose you could pull down one of these dirt roads we keep passing? We haven't seen a car yet. Nobody's going to bother us. You sleep up on the seat, and I'll stretch out in back on that canvas Clarence threw in. I sure would like to fall asleep looking up at the stars."

Pickle slowed down. He began to peer ahead down the right-hand side of the road. There was a mailbox up the road. "What's it say, Price, on that mailbox yonder?"

"It says RFD One, Loftus."

"There ain't no lights down the road you can see?"

"Nothing but darkness, Pickle."

The boy turned the pickup down the lane. A barbed wire stretched along the road on Price's side. On his side, the lane ran along the field. He pulled over and cut the lights. "We won't be bothering nobody here. We'll be up and gone before they come down the road to get their mail. You can have the seat if you want, Price, or we can take turns."

"I like it out back. I don't plan on being a country boy, so I'll just be one for now. I got my jacket in the bag. I'll be okay."

Price pushed the door open and stepped down to the ground. He was stiff. He stretched and breathed as deeply as he could. He could taste the air as he drew it into his lungs. It sure did beat riding the bus.

"The lightning bugs is out already," Pickle announced from the cab. "I didn't see none back on the farm. Seems early for them."

Dots of light flickered and faded across the field. Price had never seen anything like it. They made the darkness seem more real and a lot closer. "What are lightning bugs, Pickle? Do they sting?"

"No, they just turn on and off. You can catch a mess of them and put them in a mason jar, and they'll light up the corner of your room for a spell. Trouble is they die by morning."

Price stretched the canvas over the metal floor. He slipped into his jacket and stretched out on his back, his arms under his head. For the first time that he could remember, he felt free. As he drifted into sleep he understood that this *was* the first moment in his life when he really was free.

‖6‖

The rattle of heavy cans awoke Price from a dream about being back home. The kids on Lansing Avenue were rolling trash cans into the street. His mother was standing at the top of the stoop, shouting at Price that he'd get his bottom blistered if he so much as looked at a trash can.

He opened his eyes. It came to him that he was in the back of the pickup stretched out on a piece of canvas looking up at the first signs of another day. But the noise? It wasn't part of any dream. He sat up and looked around. Down at the end of the dirt road they had parked on last night, someone in overalls was unloading milk cans from a panel truck onto a wooden platform. It was time for him and Pickle to be on their way. They'd just say thank you and head on up the state road.

He peered in the cab window. Pickle was still asleep, his head on his jacket and his feet dangling out the door. He tapped on the window. Pickle didn't move. Price swung his leg over the side. He shook Pickle's foot.

"Not yet," Pickle grunted. "It ain't daylight yet. Tell Pa I ain't going to the field before the sun comes up."

"Come on, Pickle, wake up. I'm not your ma. We got

company, and we better move on before they take it in their head to ask us what we are doing here." Price gave Pickle's foot another shake, harder this time.

Pickle eased himself out from under the steering wheel. "What company?" he mumbled.

The panel truck started up. The driver swung it around in the middle of the empty state road and headed it down the lane. It passed by the Dodge and stopped. Pickle hadn't time to get the Dodge moving.

"You boys have a good night's sleep?" a voice called out. It wasn't a friendly voice, Pickle thought, but it wasn't unfriendly either, just curious. He turned to answer. It was a *woman,* and she was opening her door. He figured he'd better deal with her quick.

"Yes, ma'am," he answered, walking over to where the woman now stood, square and curious, beside her truck. "We pulled in here last night late to stretch out. Figured we wouldn't be hurting anybody."

"I got a sign on the pole farther down saying private property, keep out. I reckon you didn't go that far."

"No, ma'am."

"You two are hard sleepers, I'll say that for you. I came over to see what was going on. You and the boy were snoring to beat the band. You boys are a long way from home," the woman nodded at the Wisconsin license plate.

"Yes, ma'am, we are. We're headed back home now."

"It's a long way up to Wisconsin from here. Where you two boys been?" She wasn't going to let up, Price could see. He better get their story straight. He remembered that Bushnell back in the camp was always talking about his place down in Florida, where he was headed as soon as he served his time. Bushnell had come to

Lutherville to collect his wife, who had run off from him, and somehow they fell to fighting and Bushnell had busted her all up. His wife had gone on back home and was waiting there for him.

"We been down in Florida, ma'am." Just in case she asked what for, Price added, "Looking for work."

"For work?" the woman kept on. "What kind of work? The orange-picking season must be over by now."

"Yes, ma'am, that's what we found out. It was just the ragtag end and it started getting hot and we gave up and decided to go on back home."

"Lots of cows up in Wisconsin, I hear," the woman said, half to herself. "Says so right there on your license plate, 'The Dairy State.'"

Price hadn't noticed that yet. "Yes, ma'am, that's what it is, a dairy state. Lots of cows. We'll be on our way now. We thank you for letting us park along your road." Pickle turned toward the Dodge.

"Wait a minute, boy," the woman called. "You two wouldn't be wanting some work?"

"Not anymore, ma'am, thank you. We got good jobs back home. I work on the boy's dad's farm up in Wisconsin. His pa said we could go to Florida for a spell until the planting season started, yes, ma'am, that's what his dad said."

"How come the boy wasn't in school? He looks school-age to me," the woman said suspiciously.

Price felt himself sweating. He walked toward the panel truck, thinking as fast as he could. "The fact is, ma'am," he said in kind of a whisper, "the boy is a little slow. He's in what they call a special school. He keeps running away, so his dad gave up on him for the rest of the year."

"How old's the boy?"

"Sixteen, ma'am. It's just that he doesn't talk so well, not much at all, that's what his problem is."

"Is he a little touched?"

"I don't think so, ma'am. We get along just fine. He knows how to drive. They even gave him a license to drive on the state roads. Well, thank you again, ma'am."

Pickle was sitting in the cab like a cigar-store Indian, scratching his toes. "Get your shoes on now, Pickle, and let's hightail it out of here. We picked the wrong lane to park in."

"What was all that talk about?"

"About your school problems. Get a move on."

The woman walked over to the Dodge. "I'll pay you real good. I need some help. My old man got called back into the army to go to Korea. He left me with two colored boys. They weren't much good, and they took off the day I gave them their wages. Your pa runs a dairy farm?" she asked Pickle directly.

Pickle looked at Price. He nodded and bent down to lace up his boots.

"You good with cows?" she persisted. "They say people who are slow are always good with animals. The darkies had a way with our cows, I have to admit." To Price, she said, "I hope you don't mind my saying that. It's so."

"No, ma'am. I understand. I heard the same thing. Pickle here, he works with the animals. I work out in the field. Isn't that right, Pickle?"

Pickle nodded. He understood that for some reason he wasn't supposed to talk. Price would explain it to him when they were out on the road again. He had a feeling something was wrong. He hoped Price could talk his way out of it.

"You boys stay until I get some steady help, and I'll make it worth your while—a lot more than you would have made picking oranges," he heard the woman say.

"That's mighty nice, ma'am," Price responded, "but we have to be getting back about now. His folks will be worried."

"You could call them on the phone, couldn't you? Maybe his folks would say yes. Just for two weeks. I'll tell you what, I'll pay you double. A hundred dollars a week each and your keep. That's more than fair. You talk to the boy and make him understand. Will you do that?"

"Yes, ma'am. I'll talk to him for you, but I'm pretty sure he'll be wanting to be seeing his folks."

Two hundred dollars for two weeks' work! That was more money than Price had rolled up inside a boot in his paper bag, all his wages for two years' labor on the work farm. With almost four hundred dollars he could enroll in the state university when he finished high school. And Pickle would be able to show his pa that he had amounted to something after all.

"What do you want to do, Pickle?" he asked the boy, who had wiped the sleep from his eyes and finally laced up his boots. "It's a lot of money. I could use it to get me into the university."

"Sure, Price. Anything you say is all right with me. You can have my money, too. I wouldn't know what to do with that much. I got all I need to get to California."

They could argue about his trip to California later, Price thought. "I think she's a hard woman," he told Pickle, "but we both put up with your pa, and she can't be harder than he was, that's for sure."

Pickle started up the truck. "Tell her we'll follow along behind."

"Wait a minute. There's another thing you have to know, Pickle. I had to tell some lies when she was pushing me about who we were and where we were going and where we came from. I had to say you were a little slow in the head and didn't talk much. I told her you mostly nodded."

"That's okay, too. I can nod. I ain't got nothing to talk about right now, anyway."

"And cows, Pickle. What about cows? I said you looked after the cows on your pa's farm in Wisconsin, which is where we come from, because of that license plate Clarence put on the Dodge."

"Cows is cows, far as I know, unless they're beef cattle. We had a cow and her heifer for a year on the farm. We kept her for milk for Myrna, but then Ma said they brought flies to the house and made Pa sell them. 'Cept for milking, they don't take much looking after. I can show you how to milk. It ain't hard. She can't have many. There aren't many cans on the stand out there."

"I reckon we do it for two weeks, then," Price said. He walked over to the panel truck. "We'll do it, ma'am. Two weeks only for two hundred dollars for each of us. That's the agreement?"

"That's it. I'm Mrs. Loftus, Mrs. Bertha Loftus. You'll find the house and barn down the road a piece. Park out by the barn. I'll come along behind you."

Pickle pulled the pickup in to the shady side of the barn under a pecan tree. Mrs. Loftus drove the panel truck into the barn. She got out and locked the door.

"There are two bunks up in the loft the other boys used," she said. Turning to Pickle, she went on, "Unless you want to sleep in the house. We have a room in the back the handyman used when he was here."

Pickle shook his head slowly.

"Well, I'll go inside and make you some breakfast. I done let the cows out to pasture. You can start by cleaning out the stalls. I'll take your truck keys, sonny. Just in case I have to move your pickup when you're not here."

"Well, I don't know about that, ma'am. We'll be here. He'll move it whenever you want it moved," Price answered.

"He just might not be here. They'll be hanging on a hook in the kitchen whenever he needs them. There's a pump and trough at the end of the barn and an outhouse farther on."

Mrs. Loftus held out her hand for the keys. Pickle gave them to Price who gave them to the woman who tossed them in the air once and caught them to let them know whose keys they were now.

The stalls had not been cleaned in a long, long time. "Shoot," Pickle exclaimed, "if I had known this was the work, I'd of took off down the road. You get the wheelbarrow, Price, and I'll load it up. There's bound to be a manure pile outside."

"Just don't talk so the woman can hear you, Pickle."

Pickle figured he'd better get out of the habit of talking since Price claimed he was a little slow. Maybe he *was* a little slow, and that was his problem at school. Maybe Pa didn't want to tell him about it and beat his butt instead. Pa was mean enough to do something like that.

Mrs. Loftus rang a bell from the back door. She handed each of them a plate of eggs and grits and bacon.

"Leave the boy to finish the stable. He can fill the

bucket at the trough to wash the stalls down. He can wash out the milk cans when I bring them back in the morning. Tell him to be sure they're clean."

"Yes, ma'am, I will." Price said. "What you want me to do?"

"You might as well go on out to the field and get to work on the weeds, just the corn. You'll see a tobacco patch my old man put in. He got the neighbor to take care of it while he's off. You'll find what you need in the tool room in the barn. Come back at noon. I'll have your lunch."

"This is worse than the prison farm," Price muttered. "I'll get your keys, and we'll hightail it out of here."

"Naw," Pickle answered, "it ain't but for two weeks. You can put up with anything for two weeks."

It was two weeks with no days off, they discovered. Bertha Loftus told them that since they didn't have a church to go to, they might as well work on Sunday and stay out of trouble. Price scratched off the days on the wall of his bunk room, the way he had done at the prison farm. Mrs. Loftus was pretty careful not to give him a calendar, and she sure didn't invite them into the kitchen. She mainly spoke to them through the screen door. When she took off for town or wherever, she made a big show of locking the doors behind her. The only good thing Price had to say about her was that she fed them a lot better than Pickle's father.

Mostly she let them be, Price to hoe the corn and Pickle to tend the cows. In the mornings, long before dawn, they would milk the cows Pickle brought in from pasture the night before and load the milk cans on the panel truck. Pickle would clean up and come out to hoe with Price.

By the last day Pickle was itching to be on the road. He counted the scratches on the wall again as soon as they came in from the field and rinsed off at the trough. "Fourteen, Price, is that right?"

"Fourteen, that's it."

"Let's get our pay and head on out the road. Old Bertha can bring the cows in herself tonight."

Mrs. Loftus sat at the kitchen table with a Chase and Sanborn coffee can in front of her. "I don't suppose I can persuade you boys to stay on. I surely do need somebody to help look after this place."

Pickle and Price stood, waiting. "No, ma'am," Price answered softly. "We never did make that phone call. The boy's folks will be worried. And the keys to the pickup, too, ma'am. We'll be needing them."

"One thing at a time, boy," Bertha said sharply. She took a wad of bills from the coffee can and counted some out slowly, smoothing them into two piles. "Ten, twenty, thirty, forty, fifty, sixty, seventy, eight, and one, two, three, four, five, six, eighty-six dollars. That's one of you." She repeated the count, "And that's the other, eighty-six dollars each."

Pickle had a funny look on his face. "I don't think that's right, ma'am. You promised us two hundred dollars each," Price said.

Bertha Loftus turned a hard, cold face to him. "Yes, I did. But I got to thinking about it, and you boys didn't do any more work than the two boys who ran off and you ate a whole lot more. I figured I'd just have to pay you what I paid them, fifty dollars a week, and I'd have to take your keep out. That's a dollar a day, fourteen dollars. That makes it eighty-six dollars, pretty good pay for all the work you didn't do."

Price felt rage rising within him. It was just like on the prison farm, where they cheated you every chance they got. "You can't do that, ma'am. We took your offer in good faith. You're cheating us, that's what you're doing."

Mrs. Loftus turned red. "That's not talk I have to take from a darky. You mind your tongue, boy. You boys cheated me, if you want to know, that's what you did. You said this white boy couldn't talk. I sneaked out to the barn a couple of nights. Both of you was jabbering away in the loft. Funny thing, too, he talked like a cracker. Now, isn't that strange? You talk like a Yankee, and he talks like a cracker, and you're both from Wisconsin. Something's very strange, I told myself. If you don't like what I'm giving you, you go find yourself a sheriff and tell him about it. You want to do that, do you, boy?"

There was no point in Price dealing with the old woman, Pickle could see. It was like him trying to deal with Pa when he was mad about something. He wasn't going to get anywhere. Pickle took both piles of bills and jammed them in the coffee can. He gave the can to Price.

"You get me the keys to the truck and we'll take our two hundred dollars each and leave. You don't get me the keys, I'll have to look until I find them; then we leave with the whole can. You count out our money, Price. I'll help Mrs. Loftus look. I know where Ma kept things secret. I reckon she has the same places."

Furious, the woman rose to her feet. She reached behind the plates on the china shelf. She threw the keys on the floor at Pickle's feet. He bent down to pick them up. "Thank you, ma'am. You ready, Price?" Price nodded.

Pickle put the can back on the table. "Two hundred dollars each," he said, showing Mrs. Loftus the bills in his hand, "just like we agreed. Thank you, ma'am."

Out in the yard, Pickle looked up at the wires running from the pole to the house. "She ain't got no phone, just electric. She ain't going to call nobody. You get in the Dodge, Price." He headed into the barn.

Pickle joined Price a minute later. "She ain't going to go tell the sheriff for a while either. Detroit City, here we come."

|| 7 ||

It seemed to Pickle they got lost a hundred times before Price found Lansing Avenue for him. He had never seen so many streets and so much traffic. He drove slow and careful, and whenever they saw a policeman, they stopped to ask directions.

"We'll get there, Pickle, just be patient," Price told him when he complained. "Detroit is a big city. You never been in a big city before?"

"Only Lutherville," Pickle admitted. "But, shoot, Price, you grew up here. You ought to know your way around."

"After we moved to Lansing Avenue, Ma kept us as close to home as she could. She didn't want any trouble for us. Then she found out there was more trouble on Lansing than anywhere else. Turn right up there at the light, Pickle, the policeman said. The third light down is Lansing. Turn right again."

Lansing Avenue was a wide, noisy street with a few half-dead trees along the side. Cars sped up and down, burning rubber and blowing horns. Pickle crept along in the pickup until Price told him to stop in front of a big brown house behind a fence in a row of other mostly brown houses.

"This is where you live?" Pickle said, astonished. "Your ma must be rich."

"It's not ours. Ma has an apartment here on the second floor where we grew up. The folks that own it live on the first floor."

"This the colored section, Price? It don't look like the colored section in Lutherville."

"It's mostly black now. It used to be all white. It was half and half when we came here. The white folks have been moving away. Do you see any white boys on the street?"

Pickle peered down the street at the grown-ups on the front steps and the kids playing in the street. "I don't see none."

"I don't reckon you will. There used to be some white families farther down, but they must have left by now. My sister Ruth and her husband, they bought from a family who was moving out to the suburbs. Ruth lives down the street about ten houses."

Price pushed the door open and stretched his legs out toward the pavement. What would his mother say? He wished he had written from the Loftus farm, but he had a feeling Bertha Loftus wouldn't have lent him any paper or a stamp, and if he had put a letter in her mailbox she would have seen it wasn't going to Wisconsin, the Dairy State, and she would have wanted to know about that.

The woman sitting on the top step nodded. "Evening, Price. You been gone a long time."

"Two years and a couple of weeks, Mrs. Watkins. I'm home now for good. Is Ma upstairs? I reckon she's expecting me, but I'll surprise her."

The woman didn't answer directly. "You better go down and talk to Ruth. She's home. She came by five minutes ago from the store with the girls."

"Is something the matter?" Price asked anxiously. "Is she sick? Are you saying she's not upstairs, Mrs. Watkins?"

"Ruth's been expecting you every day now, Price. You go talk to Ruth. I got to go cook my supper." Mrs. Watkins stood up and went inside.

"Leave the truck here, Pickle. We'll get it later." He began to run down the street, Pickle following behind.

Price stopped in front of a house pretty much like Mrs. Watkins's. Two young girls in starched dresses and pigtails sat on the bottom steps. Price bent down to lift up the smaller. "Hi, Elizabeth. Why, you sure have grown." He knelt down to the older girl to hug her close. "You, too, Teresa. Is your ma inside?"

"I'm right here, Price." An angry voice called from above. "Right where I have been for the last two and a half weeks waiting for you to show up. Where have you been, boy?"

Pickle hung outside the wire fence. He didn't know whether to speak to the girls or not. They looked at him suspiciously.

"Where's Ma?" he heard Price ask. "She inside?"

"She's inside her coffin in the cemetery, that's where she is. She hung on as long as she could waiting for her baby, then she gave up. Where the hell were you? I went to the Trailways depot three days in a row to meet the express bus. I called the prison farm; they said you were discharged."

"Ma's dead?" Price asked, disbelieving Ruth's words. "Mrs. Watkins didn't say she died."

"I don't suppose she did, seeing as how she practically threw her out of the apartment. Said Ma owed her two months' rent. Wouldn't give us her things until George got some money last week from the savings and loan to give her."

"Ma's gone?" Price asked again, his voice choking.

"She's gone, Price." Ruth replied. She put her arm around her brother. "Come inside. Who's that boy with you?"

"That's Pickle. He drove me up here in his truck. We got delayed. You have a place for him to stay?"

"He wants to stay here?" Ruth asked.

"He's got nowhere else to stay. It's okay, Pickle. We'll find a place for you. First you better go get the Dodge and park it out front. Take the girls with you. They never rode in a county farm truck before."

"You never told me Ma had heart troubles," Price accused his sister. "I would have walked out of that camp and come straight home. They didn't have anyone watching us except Barnett, and he slept under the tree all day. Isn't that right, Pickle?"

"I reckon, but if he'd caught you, you'd of served twice your time."

George Thomas looked at Price over the saucer of coffee he was holding to his face in two giant hands. He was about the biggest man Pickle had ever seen. He filled his kitchen chair like he was sitting on one of Myrna's doll chairs. He hadn't spoken to Pickle since he came into the house, his black lunch box under his arm. He gave the box to Ruth, shook hands with Price, and took the girls on his knees. Not a word while he ate, his head low over his plate, chewing steadily until his plate was empty.

Then he crossed his knife and fork on the plate and got up to pour himself a cup of coffee. He put half into his saucer. Now he was blowing on it while he spoke to Pickle for the first time.

"Your pa a judge?"

"No, sir." Pickle shook his head. He was afraid to say just what Pa was.

Price answered for him. "His pa is the head man at the prison farm."

"That don't make no sense," George Thomas said. "What's he doing here?"

Let Pickle tell his own story, Price thought. He's going to have to learn to speak for himself.

When Price didn't respond, Pickle muttered, "I run off. I stole Pa's truck and run off. I thought I'd bring Price home to Detroit City and head out to California or somewhere."

The big man seemed interested. He sipped his coffee. "Is that what you thought? What's your pa going to say when you go home?"

"I ain't going home, sir, leastways not for a long time. Not until I'm too big for him to take the strap to."

George Thomas didn't speak. He seemed to be considering what Pickle had told him. Price explained, "His father beat him until he was sick and sent him out to the fields to work with the gang. His pa is one mean man. His ma, too, I reckon. That right, Pickle?"

Pickle nodded. "I'm going to go sit on the front steps if that's all right. I ain't never been to a city before."

"What you bring that boy here for, Price?" Ruth demanded when Pickle had left. "We just got beds for ourselves. We haven't carried Ma's things upstairs yet."

Her husband stood up. He put his plate and cup and

saucer carefully in the sink. "He can stay. I'll take the things up to the third floor. That where you want them?"

"Just the beds for now, honey," Ruth said. "I want to think about the rest."

She explained to Price that now they had Ma's furniture, they might as well rent the third floor. "There's going to be a strike in August, sure as anything, and we'll be needing the money. GM's talking tough and so is the union."

"How long was Ma sick, and how come you didn't tell me?"

"Ever since she came back from Lutherville. She told me not to tell you. She didn't want her boy to worry none down there in prison," Ruth snorted. "You and Franklin, you did nothing but cause her trouble, one thing after another. All she ever talked about was you getting into the state university, and all you and Franklin ever did was get into more trouble."

Price didn't answer right away. "Well, I'm back now," he said at last, "and I'm going to finish at the high school and go to the university. I got the money for it, almost four hundred dollars. How much does college cost, do you suppose?"

"I wouldn't know," Ruth replied bitterly. "I never went to college. You can live here with us and go back and forth if you stay off the streets. George won't put up with no trouble, you know that."

"I'm not going to cause trouble. I've had enough trouble for a lifetime before I'm twenty-one."

"And you got Ma's insurance. That's what she kept working for, that insurance and the burial society and the rent that old lady Watkins kept raising on her. The doctor, he told her to stop, but she kept on going, all the way across the city, three bus changes, to clean those rich folks' houses so they could lie around in bed and play bridge every afternoon."

Price didn't bother to ask why Ma didn't come live with her daughter Ruth and help look after her kids. Ma and Ruth never got along. His mother favored Franklin and himself. Ruth had to help bring them up while Ma was working. When they started getting into trouble, Ruth quit high school to try to keep them home. When they got worse and the law got after them, Ma blamed Ruth for it. He reckoned she had a right to be bitter.

"You take my insurance for the girls, Ruth. I won't be needing it. I'll live here and get me a job."

"Ma left me half—and all her things. You keep your money, Price, but you stay out of trouble. George won't put up with it for a minute. He'll throw you out and lock the door. And what you going to do about that boy you brought here?"

"He brought *me*," Price said. "I'm going to send him back home on the bus, that's what I'm going to do."

"Folks along the street will think it's funny seeing a white boy living here with us. They'll be teasing the girls before long."

Price knew that. He would send Pickle home tomorrow or the day after, just buy him a ticket and put him on the bus. He would leave the Dodge down the street or over on Ashatoc. Someone would take care of it.

"I can't look after him," he explained to Ruth. "It's between him and his pa."

Her reply surprised him. "He's better off looking after himself. He's safer on the road than he is getting beat every day. Let him go to California if he wants."

8

Price didn't bother to tell Pickle what Ruth had said. The boy's mind was still made up, just like it was down in Lutherville. He was determined to go to California; he planned to leave in the evening after the traffic died down. All he wanted Price to do was mark the roads on the map and put a circle around the route numbers. Pickle figured he could read numbers. When he got lost, he would ask, just the way they had done when they got lost in Detroit.

They were walking back in the afternoon from the supermarket on Ashatoc Avenue—each of them carrying a bag of Ruth's groceries and not paying much attention— Pickle, deep down, wondering if he could really take the Dodge through all the traffic in all the cities Price said got in the way between Detroit and California, and Price worrying about letting an ignorant country boy go off on his own.

"Looks like you're out of jail again, Price. Got a white dude with you for protection?"

Price raised his head. Freckles and McGee, he might have known. Trouble followed him everywhere. He took a step to the left to pass them by. Freckles and McGee took a step to their right and blocked his way.

Pickle hung behind to watch. A big yellow boy with kind of orange hair stood in front of Price. His face had some sort of ugly brown spots all over. Next to him was a little-bit smaller black boy, even meaner looking than Freckles. He laughed every time Freckles said anything.

"We been waiting for you, Price. Folks said you'd be back soon. You know why we been waiting?"

He had to answer, Price knew. Answer or not, he was in trouble. "I don't know and I don't give a damn. Get out of my way, both of you."

"The Dukes took an oath, Price, a blood feud oath to get you. You run off down South last time and hide in jail, they tell us, but we still got the oath."

"You know what you can do with your oath. Get out of my way," Price replied bravely.

"The oath is to pay you back for McGee here's brother Jonas. I might as well start now." Freckles pulled a knife from his pocket. *Click.* A blade shot out of the case. "We'll mark you up a little today to start with. Grab his arms, McGee."

Pickle watched, horrified, as McGee grabbed Price's arms. The bag of groceries fell to the pavement and burst. Pickle remembered how Pa used to brag at the supper table about how he handled the tough soldiers when he was an M.P. "You kick them where they hurt most," he used to say, "and throw them in the meat wagon." He had seen him kick a convict once when the man said something Pa didn't like.

Pickle took two steps toward Freckles. As Freckles turned to meet him, Pickle drew his right foot back. He slammed his farm boot hard into Freckles's groin. The knife clattered to the pavement. Freckles clutched his stomach. He fell to his knees and threw up. Only then did he holler, a long, hoarse howl from deep in his throat as he bent over his knees to throw up again.

Price tore himself loose from McGee's grasp to grab his enemy around the neck. McGee twisted loose and fled down the street. Price took Pickle by his arm. "Let's get home quick."

Pickle put his bag on the sidewalk. Disregarding Freckles, he picked up the scattered groceries and tucked them in his bag. He handed a carton of milk and a loaf of bread to Price. "No hurry, Price. He ain't going to bother us none."

"If you won't tell the boy, I will," Ruth said, when she heard the story. "He don't know about these things. Now you got him into trouble, too." She turned to Pickle. "He told you about Franklin?"

"No, ma'am."

"I reckoned he wouldn't. Franklin was his brother, two years older. He was in the reformatory before Price. When he got out, he took to stealing again and started this gang called the Kings, kids snatching purses and stealing from the stores and pushing trash cans out in front of cars and carrying switchblades and maybe a gun or two, for all I know."

Pickle thought of Pa's pistol in his tote bag. "They shot people?" he asked.

"Naw," Price said. "They were just showing off."

"And fighting, too, don't forget the fighting," Ruth said.

"The Kings used to fight the Dukes from over on Ashotoc," Price explained. "Franklin was leader of the Kings and Freckles was head of the Dukes."

"Where's Franklin?" Pickle asked. "In jail?"

Price shook his head.

"Don't we wish?" Ruth said. "He's dead, killed in a gang fight. Someone put a knife in him, probably Freckles or McGee. You want to tell him about the reformatory, Price?"

Price shook his head again.

"I will then," Ruth went on. "The boy ought to know about that, too. Franklin taught his brother to steal. This time it was Price got caught while Franklin ran away, just like Clarence. At least Price had the sense to give it up when he got out. He went back to school.

"Franklin, he went on fighting and stealing. Ma and I couldn't do anything with him. About the time Price was finishing his junior year, Franklin was killed. Next week McGee's brother was killed out on his front stoop one night. Ma took Price off to Lutherville to see her sister for a while. You know the rest."

"Freckles said he was waiting for me," Price said, despair in his voice.

"He's going to be waiting twice as hard now," Ruth said. "We'll wait to see what George says. Whatever he says, you do, Price. We got a family to bring up here. We don't need your troubles. You do what my husband says, you hear me?"

What George Thomas said in his soft southern accent was for Price to get his things and climb into the Dodge pickup outside and go to California. Later on in the summer when he came back, they would study what to do next.

That settled, he looked across the table to Pickle. "You done good, boy. You taught those bums a trick or two. You figure you can look after this other boy you brought home to us?"

Pickle didn't know how to answer. He shrugged and spread jam on some bread for Elizabeth and looked helplessly at Price. Price shrugged, too, and smiled to tell him he was being teased.

"We'll be all right," Price said to Ruth. "I'll be back in time for high school. I'll find me a place somewhere else in the city and go to school there."

"We'll do what the Lord has in mind for us," George Thomas said. He spoke again to Pickle. "That's a mighty fine truck your pa had. Lots of miles left on that truck. We don't make cars like that no more. Just a lot of junk is rolling off the line."

"Yes, sir." Pickle replied. "Cousin Clarence fixed it real good." If Mr. Thomas said the Dodge would take them to California and back, he was pretty sure it would. He didn't talk much, but it looked like he knew what he was saying when he did.

"Did Ma keep my schoolbooks?" Price asked his sister.

"I packed them with the other things in the basement. What do you need schoolbooks now for?"

"I can help Pickle with his lessons as we go along. Maybe they will put him in the fifth grade when he gets back if he does good."

"Looks to me like the boy already knows a thing or two," George Thomas observed. "He knows how to protect himself and drive a truck."

Ruth spoke sharply to her husband for the first time. "So do you, honey, but it sure isn't making us rich. It's the men who went to school who is running the union and GM."

"I was thinking the boy could teach Price to drive, Ruth," her husband said mildly.

"Shoot, that's easy," Pickle exclaimed. "I learned that for myself. Price can learn any old time."

Price headed down to the basement. Ma had saved his books at the end of every school year. She lined them up on the shelf in the living room. Whenever Mrs. Watkins came up for the rent, Ma showed her the books. "Price is on his way to college, Mrs. Watkins. Those books there, Price knows everything in them."

Price rummaged through the box of books. He found his fourth-grade arithmetic and social studies and reading book. I might as well take the fifth-grade books, too, although he doubted Pickle would have the patience to sit still for much learning, unless it was while he was driving the truck. He put the books in the canvas suitcase Ma had given to Ruth a long while back.

"All right if I borrow this?" he asked, showing the suitcase to Ruth. "It's better than a paper bag."

"I'm not going anywhere," Ruth said sadly. "I only used it once, when Ma went to the hospital for some treatments. You're not planning on taking me and the kids to Niagara Falls, are you, George?"

"Maybe if we win the strike," her husband answered. "We ain't making enough now hardly to live on."

Pickle had gone out to wait on the steps. Kit bag across his knees, he was trying to read a picture book to Elizabeth and Teresa. He fumbled and mumbled from word to word. Finally he gave up. There was no point busting his brain over some old words when the girls could see clear as daylight what was going on in the pictures.

"Look," he said to them. "This turtle, he can't run fast at all. The rabbit's way ahead of him." He turned the page. "Here the rabbit's taking himself a nap under a shade tree he's so far ahead." He pointed over to the edge of the page. "Here comes the turtle. Looks like he's going to catch up while the rabbit's sleeping."

"Sure he is," Elizabeth said. "He always does."

"You read this book before?" Pickle asked.

Elizabeth took the book from him. "While the rabbit was sleeping," she read, "the turtle crawled slowly by. He didn't stop to wake the rabbit up."

Pickle shook his head. "Is that what it says? They teach you to read like that in the first grade?"

"I'm only four and a half. I don't go to school," Teresa said. "Mom teaches us the words when she reads to us. What's that word, Elizabeth?" Teresa showed Elizabeth the page.

"'Rabbit,'" Elizabeth said. "That's 'rabbit.'"

Pickle stood up ashamed. They could stop in the middle of the day and Price could teach him some words and numbers. Even if he never went back home, he'd have to learn sooner or later.

He went down to stand by the pickup. Price was shaking hands with George. Then he hugged Ruth. He picked the girls up, one by one, for a hug and a kiss.

Ruth nodded down to Pickle. "Good-bye. You two be careful." To Price, she said, "Don't forget we got the telephone now. Let us know where you're at."

George Thomas lifted his hand to Pickle. "Good-bye, Pickle," he said. "Good to see you."

‖9‖

The way he figured it, Price explained to Pickle as they left the city, they had better go to Wisconsin with their license plates and get themselves some papers. He reached inside the compartment in front of him. He took out a rusty tire gauge, a handful of Neehi bottle caps, a greasy rag, and, from the back, a crumpled square of paper. Price studied it in the failing light.

"This here is the registration. It says the truck is registered to the Bedford County Department of Correction. It's got some numbers on it. They might come in handy. You be extra careful, Pickle. You got a useless registration and somebody else's license plates Clarence stole or borrowed and no driver's license. Back home maybe you can drive without a license, but you're not back home now. They do things different up here."

"Where are we going?" Pickle asked.

Price felt obliged to take charge. George's remarks about Pickle looking after him rankled. He would be twenty-one by the end of summer. He didn't want a thirteen-year-old cracker thinking he had to look after him. He'd learned a lot of things in the reformatory and the prison farm, including staying out of fights.

"Pull over under the light down there," he said. "I'll take a look at the map."

Under the streetlight, Price showed Pickle the map. "Here we are at Detroit," he said. "If we go over to Wisconsin to get things straight, we'll have to go down south and drive around the lake. It's right here, Lake Michigan, Pickle. It's mighty big. We have to go past Chicago—that's where my cousin Clarence's sister lives, but we won't mess with her—and up into Wisconsin. That's where I'll get me a driver's license. You, too, maybe, Pickle, but you look mighty young to me. You'll probably need a birth certificate or something."

"What's that?" Pickle asked.

"A piece of paper stating when and where you were born and who your folks are."

"Naw. I never saw one of them. Where are we staying, Price, near that farm you told old lady Loftus about?"

"I didn't tell her where it was," Price answered, looking closely at the map. "There's this place called Madison. It's the state capital, and they got a university there, too. Let's go to Madison to get our things done. I'd like to see a university so I'll know what I am going to someday."

"How far is it?" Pickle asked. "We better fill up the gas tank."

"I can't figure exactly. See that white route number ahead? That's Route Number Twelve. That will take us right straight into Madison, Wisconsin. Down beyond the route sign is a Richfield station. You can get your gas there."

The traffic grew thinner as the night wore on. Pickle began to think about whether Ma and Myrna missed him. He already knew about Pa. He would be saying, "Good riddance," every night at the supper table. "He'll be back like a bad penny, you wait and see. And he'll get another whipping for taking your money, Louella, I can tell you that right now. I got a lot to learn that boy."

After a while the traffic stopped altogether save for a truck or two. The lights of a big city lit up the darkness ahead. That had to be Chicago. Price had told him it was bigger than Detroit. Next to New York it was the biggest city in the whole country. But Price said they weren't going to stop. The streets were empty now. Pickle rolled his window down a little more to let the cool night air over his face. He drove on, his eyes intent for the Route 12 signs on his right. The Dodge was running like a gold watch, except for the heat pouring from the engine up through the floor boards.

Sometime in the middle of the night, not too many hours before daybreak, Pickle reckoned, the gas gauge pushed down toward empty. All the gas stations he had passed were closed, maybe a dim light on inside, but sure enough closed. Pickle pulled the pickup over to the side of the road.

Price woke up when the hum of the motor and the motion stopped.

"What's wrong, Pickle? You too tired to drive anymore?"

"I'm tired all right," Pickle admitted, "but that ain't it. We're about out of gasoline. All the stations is closed this time of night. What do we want to do?"

"What we did when we started off, I guess," Price said. "Go along slow until we find a side road or someplace we can park until the stations open. How much gas you got?"

"I don't know rightly. Pa kept the tank filled from the prison pump. I ain't never seen it so low."

"Go along until you come to the next station. We'll pull in there and park out of the way until it opens."

"What if the highway patrol comes?" Pickle asked. "They'll be wanting to know what we're doing there."

Price sighed. He had not thought of that. "Then we better find that country road."

Pickle drove slowly while Price read the signs ahead. "Madison, sixty-three miles. That's pretty close. Archer's Gas and Repairs, four miles. Can we go four miles?"

"Shoot, I can push it four miles," Pickle said.

"Rest area ahead," Price said. "That must be what we want. If the policemen come nosing around, we'll say we're resting up, just resting up, on our way to Madison. We'll snooze until the station is open."

"Hey, Pickle, what do you want from the cooler?" Price shouted.

"They got a Dr Pepper?"

Price poked around in the icy water. "Nope. Royal Crown, root beer, cream soda, Orange Crush, that's it."

"Bring me a Royal Crown. And a Baby Ruth."

The man at Archer's Gas told Price it was three-fifty for the gas and sixty cents for the soft drinks and candy.

As Price counted out the money, the man pointed to the rear license plate. "Your plate expired the end of last year. You better not let the police see that. They'll take you off the road."

"What?" Price asked. "What do you mean?"

"It's a dead plate. Look: 'Expires December 1950.'"

"Where?" Price demanded.

The man ran his finger under Exp. Dec. 50. "You're four months late. It's a wonder no one's stopped you by now. Well, thanks for the business. Come again."

"Damn that Clarence," Price swore under his breath. To Pickle's questioning look, "Clarence put expired plates on your pickup. Most likely Clarence can't read too good."

"Well, ain't nobody caught us yet," Pickle said. "All these plates are the same. Look!" He pointed ahead to the car in front of them. "You can't see what it says, only the numbers."

"You can bet Bertha Loftus saw it. She knew something was wrong. That's why she tried to cheat us."

"We'll find us a place in Madison, maybe a boarding house like Aunt Vinnie's, and park the Dodge there until we get it some new plates," Pickle assured Price.

They better get themselves a job, too, Price thought. He had left most of his money with Ruth. The money Pickle took from his ma wasn't going to last very long, and he didn't know how much they'd have to pay for the plates and his license.

Madison wasn't like Detroit. It was a big town, not a regular city, with wide streets and lots of trees and friendly-looking houses. It looked like a nice place to come and study. Price thought maybe he could come to college here instead of the state university.

"Are there any boarding houses in town?" he asked the girl at the lunch counter.

"Sure. There are lots of them. This is a college town. I live in one. But they're probably all filled up until school gets out."

"When's that?" Price asked.

"In about a month. There will be rooms free then."

"Shoot," Pickle said. "Where we going to stay?"

"You two are students?" the girl asked, curious.

"No, ma'am, we're looking for work."

"There won't be many jobs either right now." She turned a newspaper to an inside page and gave it to Price. "Maybe you can find something here."

Price ran his finger down the want ads the way he did the summer he got out of the reformatory. Down at the bottom of a column his eyes caught sight of: "Heavy housecleaning. Room and board plus forty dollars a week. Seventeen Lakeview Drive."

Price showed the ad to the girl who said, "I saw that one. I read the want ads, too. I wasn't meant to be a waitress. But I don't need room and board. Why don't you two go take a look?"

"Where's Lakeview Drive?"

"It's along the lake. It's a nice section. Mostly professors live there. You go up College Avenue to Mendota. Turn right and that will take you to Lakeview. Good luck."

In the truck Pickle told Price he knew nothing about housecleaning. Ma wasn't much at cleaning the house and she never asked him for help.

"My ma was a housecleaner all her life," Price said. "Maybe it runs in the family. The least we can do is go find out."

Seventeen Lakeview was a large dark house set way back from the street with a circular drive in front. Shaggy evergreens surrounded the house. The lawn and flower beds had run to seed. A yellow Ford sedan was parked in front of a garage at the back.

"Shucks," Pickle said, "it looks like one of them haunted houses I heard about."

"Let's go find out," Price said. "The place sure looks like it needs a lot of cleaning up."

He banged on the heavy brass knocker shaped like a whale. A boom echoed through the house. Then, from a distance, the sound of steps coming closer.

The door opened with a creak. A mild-looking fat little bald man stood in the doorway. He wore rimless glasses and a dark suit with a vest.

"We came about the ad in the newspaper," Price said. "I'm Price Douglas. This is my friend John Sherburn."

"Two of you?" the little man asked. "I only advertised for one. I guess I didn't say that exactly, did I?"

"We go together, sir."

"I guess I could use two people, as I think of it. There's a great deal of stuff I want to throw out."

Price thought of learning to drive and teaching Pickle his fourth-grade lessons. "We're farm boys, sir, and we know how to work hard. Tell you what. We'll both work half a day for the forty dollars and do some extra for the second board and keep. We need time to straighten some things out for ourselves."

"You're not from around here?" the man asked pleasantly.

"No, sir," Pickle said.

"I thought not."

"John—we call him Pickle—is from down South, sir. He's visiting his relatives on the farm next to ours. We took some time off for John to visit the city for a spell. We need a place to stay."

"Well, you're both big and strong. It's a deal. I'll pay a little more if I get a little more. Come in and take a look." He held out his hand. "I am Dr. Myron Plum. I teach at the university."

‖ 10 ‖

The house was a mess. Dr. Plum led them around the first floor, then up a dark staircase to the cluttered rooms on the second floor. He showed them two rooms at the back of the house for them to use. He pointed to a stairway going up to a third floor.

"It's really terrible up there, as bad as the garage," he told them. "My mother never threw anything away. She never cleaned the house after my father died, and she wouldn't let me have anyone in to do it for her." He paused to count the years back to his father's death. "That was twenty-eight years ago, when I was seventeen. Twenty-eight years, imagine! She never went out. I did the shopping and most of the cooking. She sat here in the house, all the shades drawn, and took in stray cats. She put food out on the back porch and left the kitchen door open. Some of them weren't strays at all. Neighbors were always coming here to take their cats back. I hated those cats. You can still smell them."

"Where's your mother now?" Price asked.

"And the cats?" Pickle wanted to know. He liked cats. Ma had got Myrna a kitten when they lived with Aunt Vinnie. It disappeared when Pa came back from the war.

He used to tell Pickle he had put it in a burlap bag with a rock and drowned it, but Aunt Vinnie said that wasn't so. The cat couldn't stand being around Pa, mean as he was, and took off.

Dr. Plum hesitated before replying. "My mother is in a nursing home across the lake. It's very nice and they look after her as well as they can. The trouble is she won't leave her chair, not even to go to bed. And the cats, John, well, I did what Mother did. I opened the kitchen door and put a lot of food on the back porch. When they went outside to eat, all nine of them, I shut the door, didn't let them back in. After a while, they went away."

They stood in the dim hallway outside the rooms assigned to Price and Pickle, each one waiting for someone to speak. The professor was the first to break the silence. "Well," he said slowly, "what I want you two to do is take everything out of the house and put it on the front lawn. Then I'll hire someone with a truck to take it away."

"Everything?" Pickle asked. "Everything in the whole house?"

"Except for my room and things that are valuable like the table silver and Mother's jewelry. Everything else, yes. I have decided to replace everything and start a new life." He paused to chew on his lower lip and think hard about something. "I have it," he said. "Bedford County, probably not far from Lutherville. Not in the town, I'd say, but not far from it, either."

Pickle had been thinking how long the job would take. He didn't really pay attention to what Dr. Plum was saying until he heard Lutherville. "Lutherville?" he repeated. "You know about Lutherville? It ain't very big."

"I have never been there, but I know where it is. It's on my map."

"You mean you know who we are?" Price asked. "Who told you that?"

"You did. I mean, John did," Dr. Plum replied, smiling. "And you just told me you were from Detroit, the west side of the city, I'd say, somewhere close to Ashatoc Avenue. But you spent some time in the South, I'm pretty certain, probably not far from where John grew up."

"Come on, Pickle, we have to go now. Thanks for the job, sir, but I just remembered something. We have to be moving on."

Pickle paid no attention. Mouth open, he stared at Dr. Plum. "You ain't been to Lutherville, not never in your whole life?"

Dr. Plum shook his head. "And I haven't been to Detroit either—well, once I did go to a meeting there for two days. No, these are places on my map."

"What map?" Price asked suspiciously. "You work for the police? I thought you were a professor or something."

"I *am* a professor, Mr. Douglas, a professor of linguistics."

"What's that?"

"It's a fancy word for language study—how you talk, the sounds you make, the sounds other people make. You know, people's speech, people's accents."

Price was thinking fast now what he had said at the front door about where they were from. He *had* said Pickle was from the South, that was okay, but he was supposed to be from Wisconsin. He hadn't fooled Myron

Plum. He had better get things straight fast, so Dr. Plum wouldn't keep after them.

"We used to live on Lansing," he explained, "until last year. That's right next to Ashatoc. We used to shop at the market on Ashatoc. Last year Pa took his retirement from the army and bought us a little farm north from here that he heard about. We got a cow and some chickens and a couple of pigs." He hoped that would be enough. All he knew about the army was what Stripes used to tell them in the work camp. He said he was a twenty-year man who couldn't stand civilian life, so he took to stealing. You could never tell with Stripes whether it was the truth or just something he made up.

Dr. Plum nodded with satisfaction. "Well, if it was this time next year, I'd probably be able to tell where you lived in Wisconsin. It takes a while for speech patterns to change. Here, I'll show you my map."

He led them to a door on the other side of the house. "This is my office," he said, opening the door to a large corner room. It was neat and clean. "You won't have to worry about this room, when you start, or the kitchen or the bathrooms. I keep them clean. It's the rest of the house I want straightened out. Come see my map."

A handmade, misshapen map covered one whole wall of Dr. Plum's office. It was made of sheets of paper he had taped together. It was dotted with hundreds of different colored pins with little tags hanging down from them. Each tag had a number, some with a letter, too, written on them.

"Here we are," he said to Pickle. He poked a finger at a section of the map. He peered at the tag. "One forty-two C." He went across to the opposite wall, where rows of card files were lined up. He pulled out a drawer and extracted a card. "Lutherville, Bedford County and environs. The rest is pretty technical. Now let's find the recording."

Dr. Plum next went to shelves between two windows. He poked around in a box and pulled out a brown record envelope. "Listen," he told them. He put a small disk on a record player. The sounds of a boy talking just like Pickle filled the room. A pause, then the voice of a woman repeating the words the boy had just spoken.

"Why, that's Ma!" Pickle exclaimed.

"Probably not," Dr. Plum said. "But it will sound like her, yes."

"How'd you get those voices," Pickle demanded, "if you never been to Bedford County?"

"Oh, my students collect them for me. My students come from all over the country. They make the recordings, and I sit in my office and do the rest. I have a very good ear and a good memory."

"Gosh," Price said. Maybe it wasn't time to move on.

"You never heard of me?" Dr. Plum asked.

Pickle and Price shook their heads.

"You never heard 'Where Are You From?—With Dr. Plum'? It was a radio show. I went down to Chicago once a week to broadcast."

"Naw," Pickle answered. "Ma only listened to the serials in the afternoon when she was home."

"What kind of a program is it, sir?" Price asked. He was certain now he wouldn't be going to the state university. He was coming to Madison to study with Dr. Plum. Imagine having your own radio program, he thought.

"'Was,' I'm afraid," Dr. Plum explained. "I had to stop before Mother went to the nursing home. For some reason it upset her to listen to me on the radio. I told her not to listen, but she always tuned in. It was just as well. People were getting bored with me after three years. They were always trying to fool me, and they never could."

"Fool you how, sir?"

"Oh, some of them would make up a fake accent to pretend they were from Brooklyn, for example, when they really came from Chicago or Denver or somewhere."

"You could tell?"

"Of course. That was the game. People would come on the program and talk and read some words I gave them. I would tell them where they came from, if they had lived there five years or more. Or I could tell where they grew up, within fifty miles. I sometimes needed that much room. If I was wrong, the sponsors would give them a thousand dollars. But they never had to. Well, I have to go to work now, and I guess you want to get started, too. It's a big job. I'll have your supper ready about six."

"Let's see what we have to do," Price suggested when Dr. Plum had gone. "Then we can figure out how long we have to stay here. The professor seems like a pretty nice guy."

"Don't forget the license plates, Price, and learning how to drive. We can use the driveway for you to learn on."

They climbed to the third floor, which turned out to be a lot of small rooms and an old-fashioned bathroom. Every room was stuffed with papers, pamphlets, clothes, bottles and boxes, empty containers—trash a quarter of a century old. Dr. Plum's mother must have started her collection here, they decided. The sharp smell of cats filled the air. Pickle tried to prize open a window. It was stuck tight.

"We'll need some tools to do that," Price said. "I'll see what they have in the cellar."

The basement was almost empty. It looked as if Mrs. Plum hadn't worked her way down to the cellar. Price found a hammer, putty knife, and screwdriver on a shelf. He jimmied the windows open and set to helping Pickle. Outside, the pile of trash mounted. Price figured it would take at least three days to clean out the small stuff before they could start to move the furniture and the heavy stuff. "This is going to take a lot of time," he told Pickle. "Afterward we have to scrub the whole place, Dr. Plum says."

"Shoot, we'll never get to California. Why don't we just take off?"

"You know why as well as I do. If anything happens and we don't have plates and a driving license, we'll end up in jail for stealing a truck. They'll send you back to your Pa, if he'll have you, and the Lord knows what they'll do to me. They may be looking for us already. It won't do me any good to say *you* stole the truck. It's the black boy who will go to jail. I'll never get to college. No, sir, we'll travel legal, or we don't travel at all. And we can use the money, too. What you going to do if something busts on the Dodge?"

"The same as they do with old horses and mules back home." Pickle laughed. "Shoot them in the head and let the buzzards do the rest. We better check on the garage."

They dumped the trash in the middle of the front circle and trudged back to the garage. They wrenched the garage doors open. Inside the dim interior, cat clutter was piled everywhere: cans, boxes, cat-food bags, wicker baskets, rags, scratched chairs, and in a far corner, the mummified remains of dead cats.

In the middle of the debris rested a big black square car. Kicking the litter out of his way, Pickle walked around the car. "It's an old-time Packard," he said admiringly. "Maybe a twelve cylinder. They don't even make them anymore, just the eight." He kicked the collapsed tires. He opened the squeaking front door and sat behind the steering wheel. He pushed the starter down. Not a sound. He tested the horn. Silence. He turned the wheel, peering ahead through the dusty windshield.

"If we had this old car, we could go to California in style. They even got a flower vase in back. This here car's a genuine antique. Climb in, Price, and we'll take off."

Price stood outside studying the different colored license plates nailed to the garage wall. They went from 1928 straight through the years down to, he saw with surprise, last year. That plate was the same as the one on Pickle's Dodge. He bent down in back of the Packard. It carried a bright new shiny 1951 plate.

He climbed inside the Packard next to Pickle. "You certain this car's not been used?"

The boy snorted, "Sure, I'm certain. We know a lot about cars, Pa and me. I knew it was an old Packard, didn't I? I kept our De Soto going most of the time." That wasn't altogether so, he knew. All he did was pump up the tires when Pa told him to and drive it over to the work-farm gas pump and fill it up once in a while when Ma didn't have any money to buy gas with. And he washed it and simonized it every fall and checked the oil and the radiator the way Mr. Jenkins at the Pure Oil station did.

But he was dead certain the Packard hadn't been on the road for a long time, maybe even since before he was born. The tires were all cracked, the upholstery was laid over with dust. "Naw, this old car's just been sitting here. Look at all the trash in back of it. Clarence could make it go if he was here. Old Clarence would love to get his hands on the wheel of this one."

"Well, Mr. Pickle," Price said sarcastically, "you kindly tell me what your antique car is doing with 1951 license plates back and front? You look at those plates on the wall—1928 right down to last year, without missing a single year. You can read dates now, can't you, Mr. Pickle?"

Pickle got out and studied the plates. They were like the ones Clarence had in his garage, but those were mostly bent and scratched. Under the dust, these plates were shiny bright, just maybe a little faded. He bent down to take a look at the 1951 plates on the Packard, "We sure can use this on the pickup. Old Plum would never miss it until we was long gone."

"We're not going to steal from the professor," Price said. Beginning to think out loud, he went on, "But we could sort of borrow it while we are here to get around town until we get our own plates."

An idea took shape as he talked, an idea that had been forming ever since Dr. Plum told them he planned to discard everything in the house and start over. "Pickle," he asked, "you know what else? All the old stuff the professor is throwing away, some of it is bound to be worth something. If we carry it on the Dodge—I mean the furniture and good stuff—I bet we could sell it and go halves with Dr. Plum. Maybe even the Packard. The professor doesn't care about anything except his map."

"He must care about the car, Price, else why did he put new plates on it every year and not take it out of the garage?"

"We'll ask him at supper time. Let's get back to work. We got a long afternoon ahead of us."

11

Pickle looked suspiciously at the three bowls of food Dr. Plum set on the kitchen table. He sniffed. He had never smelled those smells before. Whether they were good or bad he couldn't quite decide. At home Ma never paid any attention to whether he ate or not; she was too busy urging Myrna to eat. Ma's food was okay. She almost always cooked what Pa liked, and Pickle didn't have any trouble with that.

"It's Chinese food, John," the professor told him. "If you don't like it, I have lots of bread and peanut butter and canned fruit."

"It's good," Price encouraged him. "What is it, sir?"

"The blue bowl is pork and string beans with ginger. The yellow bowl is fried rice with chicken, peanuts, and red pepper. And this, in the white bowl, is a little bit of everything."

Pickle helped himself to three tiny portions. He tried the pork with string beans. It was good! So was the rice and the mixed-up stuff. He helped himself to three large portions.

Dr. Plum smiled with approval. He told them they had done a good day's work. He apologized for the sorry state of the house. He would never have got around to cleaning up, he supposed, except that he was getting married in September and had promised Gladys to do something about the stuff in the house.

"That's nice," Price said. "You going to marry a professor? I never heard of a lady professor, but I reckon there must be some."

"Gladys will be one someday," Dr. Plum assured him. "She is my best graduate student. She has an ear almost as good as mine."

"Does your mother like her?" Price wanted to know. That was pretty important, he knew. Ma had put her foot down about several of Ruth's boyfriends until Ruth brought George Thomas home. "He's a good man," Ma said. "You're lucky to find a man as good as George."

"I don't think we'll bother to tell Mother. It would upset her. I couldn't marry while she was here," Dr. Plum explained. "Anyway that's the reason for the cleanup. Gladys will take care of the decoration and new furniture when you have finished."

"There's going to be a lot of things outside," Price said. "What about if it rains? It won't do the furniture any good."

"It doesn't matter. It all smells like cat or it's scratched up. I'll call the trashman."

"You could have a sale," Price suggested, pretty certain now Dr. Plum wouldn't think much of that idea.

"No, no. I couldn't be bothered."

"Well, could we have the pieces, sir?" Price asked. "We have the truck, and we could carry it to some place where they buy secondhand stuff. We'll go halves on what we sell."

"Good heavens, no. Take it if you want and keep the

money. I'll find a store in the telephone book you can take it to. I warn you, there are no antiques. It's just the furniture Mother and Father bought fifty years ago when they moved into the house."

"How about the Packard?" Pickle suddenly asked. "It's old enough to be an antique. You might get a lot of money for it. It looks brand-new."

Dr. Plum's face clouded over. "I don't recall it was ever used. It was my father's car. Mother couldn't drive. Father was a doctor. Right after he bought it, he found out he had a bad disease that wouldn't go away. He went out to the garage one night as if he were going to see a patient, bag and all, shut the garage doors tight, and turned the motor on. Mother found him the next morning. She thought he had fallen asleep in the car."

"Phew," exclaimed Pickle. "What about that, Price? His father killed himself in the Packard. That's something and a half, that is. It's a ghost car, Price. We were sitting in the front seat of a ghost car. I knew there was something special about that car." Suddenly Pickle remembered Dr. Plum looking sad across the table. "I'm sorry, sir. I'm sorry about your father, too."

"It's all right, John. That was a long time ago. I have forgotten him. But Mother never recovered, I'm afraid. She kept waiting for Father to come home. The car had to be ready. The one thing she did, besides feed all the cats, was to get new license plates every year. In January she'd go out to the garage in her housecoat with a screwdriver and take off last year's plates and put on the new ones. For some reason, I kept on doing it when she began to forget. I nailed her old ones to the wall to let her know I hadn't forgotten, just in case she went out to the garage. I started putting the cat trash in the garage when she left it all over the back porch. The cats died and I put them out there, too. I didn't know what else to do with them."

It sounded weird to Price. But he supposed it was easier than digging a hole, especially in the winter. "Shall we do the garage, too? We'll bury the cats somewhere in the old flower beds."

"Would you?" Dr. Plum said. "That would be nice. I'll pay you extra for the cats."

"How about the car?" Pickle persisted. "Maybe we could fix it up."

"I don't think I can sell the Packard, John," Dr. Plum said softly.

"Could I have the old plates, sir?" Pickle asked. "I have a regular collection back home. I pick them up along the highway when they fall off sometimes from cars going down to Florida. I have plates from all over."

Price wanted to interrupt but decided not to. He heard Dr. Plum tell Pickle to help himself.

"What'd you do that for, Pickle?" Price asked as soon as they were out of the house. "You're going to take the new plates, too, aren't you?"

"Sure, that's what I was working toward."

"Those plates are no good without the piece of paper, the registration or whatever, to match."

"It's half of what we need, Price. It's the best half, too. I thought about it. You ain't going to get Wisconsin plates lest you can tell them about the Dodge. Any fool can see that. Like you say, I can't drive anywhere except back home without a driver's license. We'll put the Packard's plates on our Dodge and go real easy to California. If the highway patrol stops us, we'll think of something then. But I do wish I had got the car that goes with the license plates."

They removed all the papers and assorted trash from the big house and the garage in three days, just as Price calculated. It had rained the second day, and there in the middle of the circle was an enormous soggy mass which Dr. Plum promised to have a truck haul away. Pickle had worked like a demon, Dr. Plum said.

Next came the furniture. Dr. Plum had found a used furniture place, he told them, that was always ready to buy old furniture to sell to the university students.

About twice a day the professor came out of his office, not to supervise exactly, just to stretch his legs and see how the work was coming along. When he saw that Price was learning to drive, he seemed surprised. "John here has been doing the driving, has he, Mr. Douglas?" he asked, sticking his head in the window of the old Dodge. "He hardly looks old enough to have a permit."

"He says down in Bedford County—in the whole state, I guess—they don't make you have a driving permit," Price answered.

"I believe I have heard that also. It does seem dangerous to me. But now he's driving in another state. What about that? I believe he will need a license here."

"That's what I told him, sir. He's teaching me to drive so I can get him back upstate to his relatives. I never learned to drive in Detroit, and Pa's been too busy on the farm to teach me."

Dr. Plum accepted the explanation. "That's very sensible. You have to study a book of driving rules, too. I'll call up to have them send you one. And an application form. Wisconsin is a very tidy state. We all try to obey the laws here."

"It don't matter what he says," Pickle observed, when Dr. Plum had gone up to his office. "Until you're ready, I'm going to have to drive the truck to the furniture place. I'll get me a driving license here while we're about it."

Price sighed in despair. "Pickle, didn't you hear what the professor said? You have to be older than you are, probably sixteen. And you have to read a book of driving rules. You can't even read a Slow Down sign. It's all you can do to follow the road numbers. Once you learn to read, we'll see about a permit. You do *look* sixteen. And you work harder than sixteen, I'll say that for you."

"Pa always said if you took a job you had to do it right," Pickle said. "He didn't have to beat that in me. It was just the schoolwork; I didn't like the goldarn schoolwork."

After the driving lesson, Price sat on the porch swing to study the rules for an hour. Pickle kept on working. One afternoon, when Dr. Plum went to his university office, Pickle skipped out to the garage and removed the plates from the Packard. He put them on the pickup and threw Clarence's dead plates in the trash. Then he sat behind the wheel of the Packard for a few minutes. Someday, someday real soon, he decided, he would be sitting high in his rig, just like now in the Packard, highballing across the country. And maybe someday he would find himself a Packard like this one, still new, all big and black and shiny, with a flower vase and a footrest in back. He'd take Ma and Myrna over to Aunt Vinnie's any time they were ready to go.

The days sped by. Price put on a driving show for Dr. Plum. That afternoon the professor gave him a test on the rules. Price didn't miss a single question. "You have a quick mind and a good memory, Mr. Douglas." Dr. Plum congratulated him. "I predict you will do well in college. Will you enroll in the university here? You look old enough for college."

"I'm going to try," Price said. "I been out of school for a while helping us move and get started on the farm. I'm going back to school in September."

"Another thing," the professor recommended. "When you fill out the form for the license, put down you'll take the test in your own vehicle. It's easier to take the test in a car you know."

Price did just that. And he put down Seventeen Lakeview Drive as his address, but he didn't see any reason to tell Dr. Plum. He drove with Pickle to the station and parked in the lot. Pickle walked down the street a piece to watch. Price came out in a little while with a highway patrolman and led him to the Dodge. He did everything the officer told him. The man stamped the card "Approved" and sent Price back inside for his driving license.

Half jealous, Pickle said when he got in the Dodge, "I could have done all those things with my eyes closed when I was ten years old."

"You probably could," Price said. "You forget that white boys grow up learning things black boys have to find out for themselves. You think about that sometime when you're trying to figure out how to read and what two and two add up to."

The next day they made the last of eight trips to the used-furniture store. "It's good solid furniture," the owner, Mr. Rubin, admitted, "but the upholstery does smell like cats. You can never get that smell out of a sofa or a rug. If that's all of it, we better fix a price. How much do you want?"

Price looked at Pickle and Pickle looked at Price. "We don't know," they said together.

Mr. Rubin laughed. "You don't know. I could cheat you boys blind, couldn't I? I tell you what I'll do. I'll give you half of what I think I can sell it all for. That's fair enough. I won't sell all of it for a couple of years at least."

Pickle nodded. Price said fair enough, wondering what it *would* sell for.

Mr. Rubin took out a checkbook. "Who to?" he asked.

Price didn't recollect he ever had a check before. When he had jobs, he was always paid in cash. Mama did all her business with dollar bills. There was nothing he or Pickle could do with a check. "Dr. Myron Plum," he said at last.

Only outside did he look at the piece of paper. "Eight hundred dollars," he gasped. It was a fortune, he told Pickle. Now he could really plan on college.

Dr. Plum was sitting on the porch swing next to a very large woman. He introduced her as his fiancée, Gladys something or other, a long foreign-sounding name neither Price nor Pickle could make out.

"How do you do?" Gladys said without smiling. She held on to Dr. Plum's arm, waiting for them to go away.

Price gave the professor the check. "Could you turn this in for us, sir?"

"Do you mean cash it? I would be glad to." He looked at the check. "My goodness, eight hundred dollars. That's quite a lot. I'll take it to my bank tomorrow and bring you the cash."

As he went inside, Price heard Gladys ask Dr. Plum if he actually *gave* all that good furniture to two strangers. He didn't hear what Dr. Plum said.

At breakfast the professor told them he would prepare a picnic for them to take down to the lake the next day. "Gladys will be there. I'll make something very special for you. And I'll get your wages this morning along with money for the check. That will make more than a thousand dollars, a good start toward college, Mr. Douglas. John told me he wouldn't need anything back home."

Pickle was already on the third floor scrubbing the bathroom. "What did you tell the professor you don't want any of the money for? You trying to make me look cheap, Pickle?"

"I don't know nothing about money. He asked me what I was going to do with mine and for the life of me I couldn't think of nothing. I still can't, Price. You take the money and pay our way as we go along. If there's any left over, you take it to go to school. I won't use it at home, if I go home—just the forty dollars I borrowed from Ma. If I don't go home, I'll have to get me a job somewhere anyway."

Price rumpled Pickle's blond hair. "You're a good old boy, Pickle. We'll argue about it later. I'm going down to bury the cat skins. I'll be back soon to help scrub."

Price dug a deep hole in an abandoned flower patch, overgrown with weeds and grass. He shoveled the dried-out cats in, which didn't weigh any more than a handful of feathers. He looked around the garage. It was pretty clean. Pickle had dusted off the Packard. It looked lonely sitting there now on its flattened tires.

As he was closing the garage doors, Price stared at the big trunk in the back of the car. He might as well check.

He turned the handle. The trunk was locked. The first thing Price's brother had taught him out on the streets was how to pop a trunk lid in two seconds. He looked around for a screwdriver. He found a rusty one on the garage tool bench. He slipped it under the lid. He pried up hard at the exact moment he hit the trunk under the lock with his fist. The lid popped up.

Price looked inside. His breath stopped. His face turned into a look of pure terror. He forced himself to draw back from the trunk. He slammed the lid shut. He leaned against the wall of the garage, bent over trying to keep from throwing up.

He ran into the house and up the back steps to the third floor. Pickle was scouring hard at the stains in the bottom of the tub. "Has the professor left?" Price asked in a loud whisper.

"He took off for his office a while back. He told me we should make our own lunch if he's not back."

"Put your things in your kit bag, Pickle, and get out to the truck. We're leaving. Right now! Do you hear me, Pickle? I said right now!"

"What's the matter, Price? You want to go back to Detroit? Shucks, let's get our money and have us a picnic first."

Price seized Pickle's arm so hard it hurt. He dragged him out of the bathroom and down the steps to the second floor. He pushed him into his room. "You do what I say, Pickle. We're taking off now, soon as I pack. Maybe I'll tell you why someday. Maybe I won't. You're too young to know everything that goes on. Move, or I'll leave you behind."

‖ 12 ‖

Price had the door of the Dodge open and the motor running when Pickle came out to the driveway. "Get in!" he shouted.

Pickle felt a sudden stubborn urge to refuse, the way he did when Pa told him to do this or that, like weed the garden or polish the De Soto, just shouted to tell him what to do without giving Pickle a chance to answer. Once Pickle had straight out refused; he was in the garage, bent over the tractor, before he could catch his breath.

"When I tell you to do something, boy," Pa warned him, "you better do it and think about it later."

Well, Price Douglas wasn't Pa. He had no business ordering him around like he was a kid. He was the one who drove Price all the way here from Lutherville by way of Detroit. He was the one who got the money out of old Bertha Loftus when she tried to cheat them. He was the one who put Freckles on the sidewalk throwing up. Maybe he was only thirteen, but he would be fourteen on July fourth and knew how to look after things better than Price Douglas did.

He walked slowly up to the pickup. Angrily, he told Price what he was thinking. "I ain't going nowhere now," he finished. "You ain't going either. It's my truck." He reached in and yanked the key from the ignition.

Price's shoulders sagged. He leaned back hard against the seat and put his face up, eyes closed. Then he eased himself out of the truck. He looked up toward the street. Dr. Plum wasn't coming home yet. He stood in front of Pickle, who was still shaking his head with anger and muttering to himself.

"I know all those things, Pickle. You think maybe I don't know them? I can look after myself, but I have to do it my way. I can't talk to a white woman the way I want to when she cheats me. And I can't get myself into a gang war just to prove nothing at all. I may not seem much of a man to you, Pickle, but I made it through the reformatory and your Pa's work camp, and they weren't Sunday school picnics. We're friends, you and me, just like back in the cornfield, but you're still white and I'm still black, and it's going to stay that way forever.

"Right now, I'm scared," Price went on, "and I'm scared enough to admit it. I'm scared because I saw something in the back of that old Packard that told me to pick up my feet and head out of here."

Pickle remembered he hadn't bothered to look in the trunk. He was more curious than angry now. "What was it that you saw?" he asked.

"I'm not saying," Price replied. "You just have to take my word for it. You're still a boy even if you do drive a truck and talk back to Bertha Loftus and me."

"Shoot, it can't be that much. I'll go have a look. Where's the key?"

Price took Pickle's arm. "There isn't any key. I popped the lid. Listen to me, Pickle. Stay away from that old car. Maybe I'll tell you down the road if you get in the truck and leave right now."

"I ain't leaving, Price. There's nothing in the trunk that's going to scare me. I'm staying right here until the picnic, and we get all the money Dr. Plum owes us. You go on if you want." He handed Price the key to the Dodge. "You write down your address, and I'll get Dr. Plum to send you the money. I'll take out my bus fare back home. You can have the rest of the money and the truck, too."

"It's not what's in the trunk, Pickle. It's who put it there, that's why I'm scared." He saw Dr. Plum's yellow Ford turn into the drive. The professor waved to them as he drove by to the back of the house. It was too late. "Okay, Pickle, we'll stay. But we stay together, do you understand? *Together,* we stay together."

That night Price told Pickle to leave his bedroom door open. Pickle protested, but he left the door half-open before crawling into bed.

Sometime in the middle of the night Price awoke. He heard a rustling outside. He sat up on the edge of his bed and peered out the window. Someone was going out to the garage, holding a flashlight down to the ground. Price heard the garage door creak open. Silence. Then the door creaked shut. Price saw the shadowy figure walk back toward the house. He heard heavy breathing. Dr. Plum, it was Dr. Plum, he was sure. The flashlight was off. The figure disappeared into the house.

Price heard the sound of steps on the front stairs. They paused at the top. Price reached out to lift a wooden chair over his head. He tiptoed to one side by the doorway. The steps turned down the hallway toward Dr. Plum's room. A door opened and clicked shut. Price relaxed. He lay back, eyes open, listening until dawn.

It was raining when they went down to the kitchen. Dr. Plum told them he had called Gladys to postpone the picnic.

"I'm sorry about that," he told them. "I think it's going to rain all day. What I'll do is pack a basket of food for you to take with you. Would you like that?"

"Oh, yes, sir." Price said. "That's a good idea. We can get out on the road early."

"And here is your money," Dr. Plum said, handing Price a fat brown envelope. "I hope it will help you get started at the university here. If you need a recommendation, let me know when the time comes. Both of you are wonderful workers."

As soon as they drove out into the street, Pickle asked, "What were you talking about being in the trunk of the Packard? I went out to the garage while you and the professor were packing lunch. I jimmied the lid with a screwdriver. There was nothing there except some old slippers. You must have been seeing things."

Price sighed with relief. "Maybe I was, Pickle, maybe I was. But I reckon I'll sign up at the state university back home anyway."

Price drove carefully out of Madison. The cars behind him blew their horns and sped by fast, the drivers shaking their heads. "Country driver!" one of them shouted. Price paid no attention. The city behind him, he pulled the Dodge over to the side of the road. He unfolded the map in front of Pickle and himself. Wisconsin was on one side; on the other, a map of the United States.

Price studied it. "Look here, Pickle, this is a map of the whole country." He traced their trip from Lutherville up to Detroit and over to Madison. "You remember how I gave you the road numbers to follow?"

"We still got ourselves lost in Detroit," Pickle reminded him.

"That's because we didn't have route numbers. In the city, you have to know the street names. Anyway, I'm driving now, too, and you will have to do the numbers for me."

"Where's California?" Pickle asked.

Price shook his head in despair. "Where do you think? Right out there at the end of the country where you can't go any farther. That blue there is the Pacific Ocean. Did you figure on getting to California by yourself?"

"Never mind. I would of got there. I know about the Pacific Ocean. Pa went there on a boat after he beat the Germans. He said it took three weeks. He made a lot of money rolling dice."

"What else do you see on this map in front of you?" Price asked.

Pickle peered down at the map. "A lot of lines and words. I know the numbers."

"But not the words, eh, Pickle?" Price asked. "Didn't they teach you anything in that school? Nothing at all?"

"I reckon they tried to, but I wasn't paying attention."

"You better pay attention now. We have a long way to go. Look, here we are and this is California, and in between is a lot of plains and the Rocky Mountains. I bet you heard of them sometime?"

"Yeah." Pickle replied. "Indians and grizzly bears. I heard about them."

"Good. We can take a look at the mountains. Okay, follow my finger here in Madison out to the Pacific Ocean. All those roads have numbers. See if you can find a line with the same number that goes all the way out there."

Pickle bent over the map. There weren't so many lines going out to California as there were in back of Price's finger. There were hardly any lines at all in some places. As far as he could see, only one road seemed to keep its number all the way out to the blue space that Price said was the Pacific Ocean.

"Look here, Price, number twenty goes all the way, ain't that so?"

Price looked where Pickle pointed. Route 20 made a lot of twists and turns and went up and down on the map, but it kept on going until it ended at the ocean in Oregon at a place called Newport. From there it was a long way down to Los Angeles.

"I don't know, Pickle. Maybe we ought to take Route Twenty to the Rockies and figure out another road to California from there."

"I got us a road, Price, without any help," Pickle said proudly.

"You sure did. See, you've learned something already, how to read a map. What we're going to do from now on, Pickle, is teach you other things as we go along so you'll be ready for the fifth grade."

"I don't know, Price. I can drive a truck, and now I can read a map. That's all I need. I ain't no account in a schoolroom. I don't reckon I'll ever learn."

"Yes you will," Price insisted. "The first thing to do is stop saying 'ain't.' That tells everybody you are an ignoramus. My ma never went to school a day in her life, but she knew that much. She wouldn't let Ruth and me say 'ain't.' We had to talk proper."

"'Ain't' is the way Pa speaks," Pickle objected.

"Look at your pa," Price replied. "All he's good for, seems to me, is taking the strap to you and bossing convicts. Is that what you want to be, Pickle? Isn't that what you're running away from?"

"You won't be hard on me if I don't do good, Price? You promise?"

"I won't be hard on you, because you are going to learn. Anyway, it's 'do well,' not 'do good.' I'll do most of the driving for a while, and you do the studying."

"Nah-uh," Pickle protested. "It's my truck, and I'm going to do most of the driving."

"How many times are we going to fight about this? It's the county's truck, not yours. You just stole it. Once we get to California, we're turning around and you are taking it back where it belongs. I don't see that they'll put you in jail, since your Pa runs the jail. I'll tell you what, Pickle. You drive the big stretches out in the country. Nobody's likely to stop us on the highway if we don't go too fast. If they stop you when you're driving in one of these towns because you don't do what the book says, you with no license and the Dodge with no registration, we'll both be in trouble, me more than you."

"You can say you was hitchhiking, and I gave you a ride," Pickle told him.

"I can tell them I'm Snow White, too, and you're one of my dwarfs. I got a record, Pickle, a record of being an accessory to car theft. Let's do it my way for a while, agreed?"

"Okay," Pickle grumbled. "But when we get to them mountains you found on the map, I'm doing me some driving, I don't care what you say."

"*Those* mountains, Pickle."

"Those mountains." Pickle sighed. "You know what I meant."

‖13‖

"Just read what it says," Price told Pickle. "You know your letters, don't you? Sound the word out. If you can't do that, spell it out for me."

"Shoot, Price, far as I can see, this is a dumb book. It ain't telling me nothing I want to learn."

The road lay straight in front of the pickup, straight as an arrow, through fields of young corn. Price noticed no one was working the fields. He wondered how they kept the weeds from creeping in between the stalks. The fields stretched into the horizon. It was more corn than any work gang could take care of. Maybe they had some kind of machine to do the work.

His attention snapped to Pickle's lessons. He had to correct Pickle. "'It isn't telling me anything,' not 'It ain't telling me nothing.'" he said.

"It isn't telling me anything," Pickle repeated sullenly. "Do I have to go on reading this stuff about the Pilgrims?"

"It's all I could find in my fourth grade books," Price explained. "It's learning to read, not liking the story. I used to think the Pilgrims didn't have much to do with me, either. I reckon my folks way back then were in Africa, not up in the woods eating turkey with Indians. I never saw I had much to be thankful for, but Ma said I should be thankful to God for just being alive. She always got a turkey for Thanksgiving from one of the women she cleaned house for. A real big one. Man, I got tired of turkey sandwiches."

"We always went to Aunt Vinnie's. What did Pa give you in the bunkhouse?"

"Same as always, a piece of pork, grits, and greens. Same on Christmas, too. Your Pa didn't take to coddling convicts. Now, go on reading, Pickle. I'll be asking you questions once you're done."

"'When the ha, ha, H-A-R-V-E-S-T'—what's that spell, Price?"

"'Harvest.' You know what that is, don't you?"

"Yeah. 'When the harvest was in, the Pilgrims de-ci-ded, decided, to in-vite the Indians to eat with them. The Indians came, br, br-ing—'"

"Bringing," Price helped.

"'Bringing food with them. This was the first . . .'" Pickle paused, studying the long word at the bottom of the page. His lips moved silently. "'Thanksgiving,' I think it says. 'It is a H-O-L-I-D-A-Y.'"

"Holiday."

"'Holiday?' I have trouble with the *h*'s," Pickle complained. "'A holiday Americans cel-e-brate down to the present.' Period! Did I do good, Price?"

"You did very well, Pickle. Tomorrow you'll read about the revolution against the British. Get started with your arithmetic."

"Subtraction?"

"Subtraction. After that, you'll learn multiplication and division. That's as far as I ever got in arithmetic, it seems like."

Pickle started to mutter the figures. They weren't all that hard. The numbers looked sort of familiar. "Where we going to spend the night, Price?" he asked. The night before, their first night on the way west, they had found a road going into a state park that was closed. Pickle said it was his turn to sleep in back. They had thrown a mattress in back from Dr. Plum's junk pile. The trouble was it had rained and leaked through the canvas Pickle had spread over the mattress.

"It's my turn in back," Price said.

"What if it rains again? It looks like rain."

"Then I'll get wet, just like you did," Price laughed. "It's a warm rain. I'll double up the canvas."

Pickle remembered that Pa used to tell them every once in a while that a tramp or a hitchhiker had come by the farm asking for a bunk to spend the night on. Pa sent him to the jail in Lutherville. "Those bums got a right to ask, I guess," he said, "just like I got a right to say no. Let the sheriff look after them."

"We could sleep in a jail house," he told Price. "They're supposed to let you in if you ain't got—I mean, don't have—any money. Anyway, that's what Pa said."

"I've slept enough in jails," Price responded. "Three years of sleeping in jail is enough for me. I'd rather be wet."

"Yeah. We could try at least," Pickle said. "It ain't going to do no harm."

Price didn't bother to correct him. Pickle was learning pretty fast after only two days; there was no need to discourage him. "What do you suggest we do, just knock on the jail door and ask for free bunks?"

"Sure," Pickle replied. "We can tell them a story, like we did to Bertha Loftus."

"You saw how well that worked, didn't you?"

Pickle ignored Price's remark. "We can say you're giving me a ride out to my grandmother's in California because my folks is both dead. How about that?"

"Why aren't you taking the Trailways or the Greyhound? What's a black man doing carrying a white boy to California?"

"I can say you lived down the street and was going west to look for work, and I gave you the bus money to carry me, but it ain't enough for a hotel and we've been sleeping in the truck, but it looks like rain."

"That's not going to work, Pickle; let's hope it doesn't rain."

But it did rain. It came down in sheets late in the afternoon. Pickle got his back up. "I ain't going to sit all day in the front seat and sleep there at night, too, Price. And I ain't—I mean, I'm not—going to sleep in the rain. Find us a jail. We'll ask real polite. Maybe they won't ask us no questions back."

"They ask us *any* questions, Pickle, we turn around real polite and leave, agreed?"

Price turned off the highway at the next town. He drove down the rain-drenched main street. Toward the far end where main street started turning into a country road, they came to a brick building. Letters carved in a granite block over the door told them it was the courthouse. A police car was parked at the side of the building.

"The jail must be out back," Price said. He pulled the Dodge to the curb. "Are you sure you want to do this, Pickle?"

"Keep on going," Pickle told him. "Go down the

street and turn around. Then let's go up and down the streets where's some houses."

"What are you talking about, Pickle? The jail you wanted is right here."

"Yeah, I know, but I've been thinking, Price. We ought to be hitchhikers. If we show up in a truck, they might think we got enough money to buy us a place to stay."

"You're pretty smart for a country boy, Pickle," Price said.

"Most country boys are pretty smart, so long as they stay in the country." Pickle laughed.

Price found a quiet street where the houses were set back in their yards and pretty far apart. Some cars were parked in driveways; others were out on the street. He parked the Dodge in front of an old roadster.

Pickle grabbed his kit bag and took Price's suitcase from under the canvas in back. They walked out to the main street and past the darkened storefronts to the courthouse. Down back of the courthouse was a shining light bulb over a screen door. Moths were fluttering around the bulb. Price knocked cautiously.

A voice called, "It's open. Come in."

A big man in a tan shirt with a badge and a straw hat cocked back on his head was seated at his desk. He was cleaning a pistol with an oiled cloth. "Howdy," he said. "Looking for a room?"

"Yes, sir," Pickle responded.

"Thought you might be. That's why I stay here until dark. Lots of people walking the roads this time of year. You men looking for work?"

Price shook his head. "Maybe farther along."

"We're going to California," Pickle butted in.

Before he could continue, Price spoke up. "It didn't look like we were going to get a ride any farther tonight."

"No, I reckon not," the man replied. He gave the pistol a final rub and slipped it into the holster at his side. He stood up. "I don't have any residents out in back right now. Help yourself."

"Thank you, sir," Price said. "We're much obliged."

"No matter," the sheriff said. "I figure if we can't help folks along, we shouldn't be here. My wife will give you breakfast. Take the car path outside to the white house across the field. I'll get on home now myself."

There were six cells in the jail block, each with its barred door open. A blanket was spread over each bunk, a clean white pillow at the head.

"Shoot," Pickle said. "We done pretty good, didn't we? It's a lot better than Pa's bunkhouse, ain't it, Price?"

"Shh, not so loud, Pickle."

"Well, it is, ain't it?" Pickle asked again. Price's assurance was important to him.

"Yes, it certainly is . . . but," he came close to Pickle and whispered, "it still smells like a jail. You couldn't get the smell out, unless you blew it up with dynamite."

Pickle sniffed. "I don't smell nothing."

"'Smell anything,' Pickle. Well, I do. You never did time. A jail house or a reformatory or a prison or a bunkhouse—they all smell the same. They stink. Which room do you want?"

"I'll take this one," Pickle said, carrying his bag into a middle cell. "It's got a window open up there in the wall."

The sound of a dog barking furiously awoke Price. Instinctively, like on the work farm when the get-up bell rang, he swung his legs over the edge of the bunk and pushed his feet into his boots. He rubbed his eyes. Pickle was on is back across the way, snoring heavily. He went through the sheriff's office to the outside. The sun was clearing the horizon. Car tracks cut across the wet grass on the field toward a plain white house. A dog was chained to the shed, howling to the skies. The back door of the house opened. A woman brought the dog a pan of food. It shut up.

Back inside, Price shook Pickle by the shoulder. "Let's go for some breakfast, Pickle, and get out of town before folks begin to stir."

Pickle struggled to his feet, grumbling. He stumbled into the sheriff's tiny bathroom.

"The sheriff said you might come over for breakfast," a friendly woman in a housedress said when she came to her back door. "Come on in. Be quiet, you two," she said to a pair of blond-headed boys who were banging on the table with their spoons. "Twins." She shook her head in despair. "Folks said twins would be easy, but they sure never had any."

One of the boys stopped banging his spoon. He looked long and hard at Price. "You are black," he declared.

"I reckon I am," Price answered, smiling. "What are you?"

"What am I, Mom?" the boy asked his mother.

"I guess you are a rude little white boy, Bobby." To Price, she said, "I'm sorry. I don't think Bobby has ever seen . . ." She stopped, turning red.

"A black man," Price helped her. "There don't seem to be many of us out here. Bobby has something to tell his friends."

Still flustered, the woman turned to the stove. "Ham, eggs, toast, and coffee, that all right with you?" she asked.

"Yes, ma'am," Pickle said. "We'd like that fine." Price had told him not to talk much, but he could see Price and the woman were having troubles.

The woman sat at the end of the table sipping from a cup of coffee while she watched them eat. "Lots of men are coming through now. Sam and I try to help them along. They say it's going to be a good year for corn and wheat. The farmers will need a lot of help."

"We're going to California," Pickle said. "Leastways, we plan to go there if we can get enough rides."

"Where you men from?" the woman asked.

Before Price could answer, Pickle spoke. "Wisconsin, ma'am. Madison, Wisconsin."

The woman was silent for a while. "You talk sort of funny to be from Wisconsin," she said. "You talk like you're from down South."

This time, Price was quick to answer. "That's what everyone says about John. That's where he's originally from. He still talks that way, even after a couple of years up North."

The woman nodded. "I was right, then. Sam is supposed to be looking out for a runaway boy—or maybe he was stolen—from somewhere down there. Light hair, thirteen-fourteen years old. That's what the bulletin said."

"I'm sixteen, ma'am," Pickle said. "I don't reckon that's me."

"We better get on the road, John," Price said. "The trucks will be coming through about now. We've had pretty good luck with trucks so far," he explained as he pushed his chair back. "Thank you for the breakfast. You two boys look after your mother. Good-bye, ma'am."

"Me, too, ma'am. I mean, thank you. And thank the sheriff for the bed." Pickle followed Price down the back steps and across the field. When they were beyond the courthouse they broke into a run.

14

"That was you she was talking about, Pickle," Price said as he tried to start the Dodge. The motor was wet from the rain. It kept dying.

"Pull out the throttle," Pickle told him. "Sometimes that works."

The pickup started. Price breathed with relief. "You said your pa wouldn't bother to look for you. He must have sent out a bulletin. Looks like they want you back, after all."

"Ma and Aunt Vinnie must have kept after him. He wouldn't have done it on his own. I reckon we better stay out of jails for a while."

"I reckon we had, Pickle, just like I said to start with. You know, sometimes you're right, but sometimes I'm right, too."

"She didn't say nothing about the Dodge."

"That doesn't mean the bulletin didn't say. You and the Dodge disappeared the same time. And what about that doctor that came along down the road from Lutherville? By now they may have figured I kidnapped you."

"The sheriff would have us both in the jailhouse if

they was looking for you, too, Price. I was pretty smart to park the pickup here, wasn't I?"

"And I was pretty dumb ever to listen to you," Price said. "Give me the map. We'll find some back roads to run on for a while."

Price took the map. He pulled over just before the street came onto Main Street. He saw the sheriff's car speed by toward the highway.

"Where do you think the sheriff is going in such a hurry?" Price asked. He studied the map. "If we go back down past the courthouse that road turns west. Then it connects with another road that doesn't have any number. We'll go along these country roads and stay out of towns when we can for a couple of hundred miles. Like you say, Pickle, we aren't in any hurry. And if we have to talk to someone, let me do the talking. That cracker accent makes you stick out as much as my black face."

It was slow progress along the small country roads. Sometimes it seemed they were going backward more than forward. They had to follow tractors and trucks and farm machinery for miles without a chance to pass. Once a day Price would stop in one of the small country towns. He slumped deep behind the wheel while Pickle went in the store to buy them a loaf of bread and half a pound of balony and soft drinks. Pickle used the little speech he practiced with Price.

"And don't say much else," Price warned. "Get our food and get out."

At dusk they pulled deep into a dirt track that divided the fields, a road for farm machinery, they were pretty certain, not a road to a distant farmhouse. After they ate, Price leaned back against the cab and lighted his cigarette for the day. He stared up at the evening sky and relaxed his muscles.

"Where do you reckon the sky goes?" he asked the boy.

"There ain't no end to it," Pickle replied. "'There isn't any end to it,' I mean. It's like the multiplication table. It just keeps on going. There's no end to those numbers, is there, Price?"

"They go to infinity, I guess, just like the stars up there."

"And the words, too, I mean the letters. I counted them up. There are only twenty-six of them. Some don't count for much, like *q* and *z* and *x*. If it wasn't for the zebras, they wouldn't have no use for the *z*. But, I've been thinking, Price. Them—*those*—letters is like the numbers, they go on forever, you can keep making words until you drop and you ain't—*haven't*—half begun."

Price had never thought of it that way. Pickle was right. Every once in a while, he realized, this dumb country boy had ideas that surprised him. Still, he'd rather think about the stars, and the sky that was both everywhere and nowhere. Out here in the fields where there was no light and the only sound was the corn rustling and the nighthawk whirring past, the sky reached down to envelop him. Later when he tried to explain how he felt to Pickle, the boy always said, "Shoot, Price, it's just infinity or whatever you call it."

Pickle had learned more in school than he let on. They were already on Price's fifth-grade books. What they would use when they finished those, Price didn't know. Back in Detroit, it hadn't occurred to him that Pickle would learn so fast—or, maybe, that he was such a good teacher. Whatever, they would be through with the books he brought by the time they reached California. Price supposed he could buy some books in Los Angeles, which was where Pickle was determined to go. His mother was always talking about the movie stars. Pickle figured if he saw one or two to tell her about when he got home, she might tell Pa to stop walloping him.

The roads began to rise. You could feel them going up. The map told him they were getting close to Wyoming. The grain fields turned to grazing plains and woodlands. The air was crisper, even at the high noon hours when the heat rose off the asphalt in front of the Dodge. Price was amazed at the never-ending expanse of the land.

"It ain't like Lutherville," Pickle said. "Even when you didn't see anybody at home, you knew someone was around. Out here, you can't be sure if anybody is around or not. It sure is big. It makes you feel like you was an ant or something, don't it, Price?"

"Yes, it do," Price teased him. He unfolded the map again to study where they'd been and where they were headed. The back roads were getting scarce. Soon they would have to take Route 20. They had stopped counting the days. It must have been almost a week since they slept in the jail.

"We're in Wyoming now," he told Pickle.

"The Rockies are out there, you said, Price. Show me again."

Price put his finger on the mountains. "Shall I put a pencil mark around them for you?"

"Let me do it?" Pickle asked. "Don't forget, Price, that's where I'm doing the driving. Ain't nobody going to be looking for us in the Rocky Mountains, that's for goldarn sure."

Price didn't bother to correct him. Pickle knew how to talk now when he put his mind to it. But when he was excited, all his Lutherville talk came back and he sounded, it occurred to Price, like one of those funny voices on Dr. Plum's talking machine. If he listened to himself now, Price could hear himself talking just a little bit like Pickle. The trip to California was changing both of them. He watched Pickle draw a heavy pencil line around the mountains. He laughed to himself. They weren't the same two people who stole out of Lutherville many nights ago, no siree, that was for goldarn sure.

"Durn it, Price, you going to take all day looking at those maps? When you ain't driving, you're studying maps. When I ain't driving, I'm looking at books. Shoot, what kind of vacation is this? All we got to do is follow Route Twenty, you said."

Price put his finger on a place on the map and looked up. "Well, Pickle, I ain't never had me a proper vacation before, like going over to Aunt Vinnie's for Sunday dinner or to the picture show on Saturday night, so I have to figure out where I'm going by studying the maps."

"Aw, come on, Price. You got no call to tease me. I just want to get up in the Rocky Mountains and do some driving. You've had all the fun on this here trip."

"Like driving down back roads behind manure spreaders, listening to you learn to spell. You call that fun, Pickle? I've had more fun in the work camp playing checkers."

Price was angry, Pickle could tell. So was he. Neither one of them knew where they were going. They were tired of balony sandwiches and hot sodas, tired of long dull days between the cornfields and the cow pastures. He was reading a lot of dumb things in a book that neither he nor Price was interested in. They did need a vacation. He wasn't sure exactly what it was. Ma nagged his father in the summer about going down to Florida for a week or two. Pa never paid her any mind. His idea of a vacation, Ma said, was his two weeks reserve duty at the army camp while she and Myrna stayed home.

"I'm sorry, Price," he muttered. "Why don't we find us a nice place and camp out for a while? Nobody's looking for us out here."

"I was thinking the same thing," Price said. "Take a minute to look at this map the man gave us at the Seventy-six station. Here we are outside this town called Shoshon. Right here, you see, good old Route Twenty takes off up north."

Price moved over to the tattered map of the United States spread on the hood next to the map of Wyoming. "Like I told you when you found us Route Twenty, it comes to the ocean a long way north of Hollywood. I reckon we don't want to follow Twenty anymore."

"I don't care," Pickle answered. "All I want is some driving and getting to California. How are we going to do that?"

"The way I figure it, we switch over here to Route Twenty-six. It goes through this Wind River Indian Reservation ahead of us right up to the big mountains. The Grand Tetons, they call them, fourteen thousand feet high. Phew, think of that, Pickle. That's almost three miles high."

"Is a reservation where they keep the Indians, Price? You reckon we'll see any?"

"I think it's the land the government let them have to live

on. It's probably not much good if the government let it go. There was an Indian in the camp when I first got there. He came from a reservation down in Florida. He got drunk and stole a car and ran into a school bus in Lutherville. He said the reservation was worse than the work camp. They sent him back when his term was up. Sometimes I think that's what they'd like to do to us, too."

"What's that?" Pickle asked.

"Put all the black people in a reservation and throw away the key."

"That's what Pa says," Pickle told him. "They going to do it?"

Price shook his head and bent over the map again. "We take Route Twenty-six," he explained to Pickle, "to where it crosses Route Eighty-nine. There's a lake up there under the mountains, and a couple of little towns. Afterward, Route Eighty-nine will take us on down toward Los Angeles."

"Can we make a fire and catch fish and live like the Indians who were friends to the Pilgrims, is that it, Price, like we read in your fourth-grade book?"

"Maybe we'll climb the mountains, too," Price said. "Wouldn't that be something?"

"Can I drive all the way now?" Pickle asked.

"As soon as we get to"—Price looked at his map—"as soon as we get to some place called Crowheart."

The road curved and twisted higher. Mountain peaks rose toward the sky. There weren't many cars on the road now, more often than not an old pickup like the Dodge, or older, driven by a brown-faced man with maybe a couple of brown-faced black-haired kids in tattered shirts leaning out the back.

"Indians, Pickle, you wanted to see some Indians."

"How come they aren't wearing feathers? Shoot, they look just like us. And that's an old Dodge just like ours. Why ain't they riding horses?"

"They're Americans just like us, Pickle—probably more like me than you," Price said bitterly.

Crowheart was a little town at the edge of the road. Indians were sitting on the front steps of stores, just like the farmers sat on the steps of the general store and drugstore in Lutherville, Pickle thought, sitting there all day long spitting tobacco juice on the sidewalk. He stuck his head out the window and waved. The stone-faced men in Crowheart did not wave back.

A sign told them the Wind River campsite lay to the right. Price turned onto a dirt road that carried them to nearly empty stream bed. Willow trees and poplars leaned over the green banks. Price pulled up the handbrake. He handed the key to Pickle. "Here's your truck back." Price realized how hungry he was.

"Pickle," he said, "we forgot to get our food back there in Crowheart. Why don't you go to town and buy us a steak and some crackers? Maybe a pan or two and some knives and forks and coffee and a coffee pot and, oh, yes, a canteen. Get me a pack of cigarettes and some beer. I'll lie here under the trees. I'll cook up a supper later."

"I got us a couple of straw hats, too, like the Indians wear," Pickle said as he dropped the cigarettes on Price's stomach, "and all the other stuff you asked for. No beer. The Indians aren't allowed to have beer or nothing."

"I guess black people aren't either, then." Price sat up. He felt warm and rested. "What did you get, RC Cola and Dr Pepper?"

"Same as always," Pickle said. "I'll go bury them in the stream."

Price and Pickle sat under the trees and stared in wonder at the horizons. "It sure ain't like back home," said Pickle. "Them Indians ought to be grateful to the government for giving them a place like this."

"What're all those 'ain'ts' and 'thems,' Pickle? I thought I had you cured."

"I know, Price, but it's hard for me to remember all the time. When I'm tired, it's just easier to talk the way God meant me to talk."

"God didn't have anything to do with it," Price said. He stood up. "Let's build a fire down on the sand. I'll see what I can do with that piece of meat."

15

The road to Jackson Lake was a narrow winding strip that climbed upward between plunging gorges and ragged mountainsides. The valleys were dark with spruce and fir. The air was chill. Pickle pulled at the heater knob. Nothing happened. "Damn," he muttered.

The boy leaned forward over the wheel. A misty gloom had descended over the road. Once in a while a car or pickup came down, lights on and horn blaring as it made the turns. Driving wasn't as much fun as Pickle had thought it would be. He peered over the edge of the road to his right. It was a sharp drop down to the rocks and trees below. If the Dodge blew one of its front tires, they were goners. A white roadside sign told them they were passing over the Continental Divide.

"What's that sign say?" Pickle asked.

"It says you are at the Continental Divide. I don't know what that means. Maybe we'll find out later."

The rain began, drizzling at first, then coming down steady, and, finally, slashing in sheets across the windshield. Pickle could not see the road. He turned the lights on. There was a dirt patch under an overhang ahead on the left. He pulled under the rock shelter. "If the motor gets wet, we won't go anywhere until it dries out," he complained to Price.

Minutes later a heavy roadster, canvas top up, parked behind them. When the downpour slackened, a man got out. He pulled his raincoat collar to his hat brim and came up to Price's side of the truck. He tapped on the window. Price lowered it.

"Do you need help?" the man asked.

The man looked rich. He smelled faintly of shaving lotion. Price was very polite. "No, sir, we stopped for the rain to pass. We didn't want to kill the motor."

"That was wise. These storms in the mountains usually don't last long. Well, good luck to you."

"How far is it from here up to the lake?" Price asked.

"Jackson Lake? There are other lakes at Jackson Hole."

"Just a minute, sir. I never heard of Jackson Hole." He quickly unfolded his map. "Here," he pointed. "This is where we want to go. We figure on camping a couple of days."

The man took his hat off and put his head in the window. "This whole area is called Jackson Hole. Now it's a national park, Grand Teton National Park. See, this is the mountain range. The biggest mountain is Grand Teton. The lake below is Jackson Lake. The other lakes are smaller. Some of them aren't on your map."

Pickle leaned across to ask if there were any towns.

"Jackson is the biggest, and it's really quite small. It's pretty empty country. If there's anything else you need to know, you can ask at the ranger station where you turn into the park. It's not far now."

The man went back to his car. A chauffeur got out and opened the door for him.

"Well, would you look at that, Price. He's got himself a regular driver in a uniform. Ain't that something?" Pickle watched the big car roll out onto the road and disappear. "'Course you got a driver, too, Price—me."

Half an hour later a board with carved letters announced that they had come to Grand Teton National Park. In back of the sign was a wooden hut. As the Dodge appeared, a man came out of the hut.

"Where you fellows going?" the ranger asked.

Pickle opened the door and stepped out. He arched his back. "Camping, I reckon. We aim to find a lake and fish and maybe climb a mountain or two. That right, Price?"

The ranger smiled. "We have a lot of lakes and mountains, and there are a lot of fish in the lakes." He looked in the back of the truck. "Did you bring a tent with you?"

"We've been sleeping in the back or up in the cab, officer," Price said. "And in jails, a couple of nights when it rained."

"I'm not an officer, just a park ranger. But I can't let you camp out like that here. You need a tent between you and the bears."

"Bears, real live bears?" Pickle exclaimed.

"I'm afraid so. Wolves, too, but they won't bother you. If the bears get excited, they can be dangerous. They killed a camper last year."

"Shoot, all this way to camp out, and we're out of luck. What are we going to do now?"

"You might want to buy a tent," the ranger said. "They sell them at the store in Jackson. In a couple of years we'll have cabins for visitors, like up in Yellowstone, but we just opened the park here. There's a hotel down in Jackson and a little motel. They're both probably filled. I'm sorry."

"Let's go see, Price," Pickle said. "We haven't spent any of our money yet, except on gas."

"Good luck." The ranger saluted with two fingers to the brim of his Boy Scout hat. "Of course, you might stay with Senator Phelps. He has a big ranch house. I'm just teasing you."

"Senator Phelps?" Price asked. "Who's he?"

"He owns a lot of Jackson Hole—or he used to. He sold most of his land to the government for the park. He came in just ahead of you."

"He did?"

"Yes. Tan roadster. Maybe he passed you."

The senator had been polite enough, Price remembered, but he sure hadn't invited them to stay with him.

"Ask him about the sign, Price," Pickle said.

"We saw a sign back down the road that said Continental Divide. What does that mean?"

"It means that at that point all the rivers in the country drain one way or another. In back of you, they flow down to the Gulf of Mexico or into the Atlantic. Right here on the other side of the divide, they flow toward the Pacific. The Snake River runs into Jackson Lake and out again and turns west. It's one of the big rivers out here, that and the Colorado."

"Thank you, sir," Price said. "We'll head on down to Jackson."

"Sorry I can't help you. Here's a map of the park. Remember, I was serious about sleeping out in the open."

"Bears!" Pickle almost shouted. "Did you hear him, Price? Bears! And wolves, too! Did you ever?"

After the downpour, the dirt road was a mud track. The Dodge slithered and skewed in the ruts. Through the branches they saw the dark outlines of an occasional cabin. They passed along the edge of pasturelands. Smoke rose from the chimney of a distant ranch house.

It was almost dark. Pickle turned the headlights on. He swore to himself as the ruts pulled the wheels this way and that. They passed through a cluster of houses that Price said was called Moran and another cluster that was a place called Moose. "It's Jackson we want," he told Pickle. "It's still a good way to go."

They came at last to a larger cluster. Cars and trucks were parked in front of buildings. Lights shone from windows. Loud shouts and the sounds of a radio came from the hotel, an old frame building.

The clerk at the desk told them they had no rooms free. He understood the motel was also filled.

Price sighed. "I'd like a bottle of beer before we move on," he said to Pickle. "We'll celebrate getting this far. There are other parks we can go to without any bears." He headed into the bar.

"A bottle of beer and a cola for the boy, RC," Price called to the bartender.

The man behind the bar looked hard at Price. He wiped his hands on a white apron. He started to say something and changed his mind. "What kind of beer do you want?" he asked.

"Whatever you got," Price answered, "so long as it's good and cold."

Pickle turned his back to the bar. At the end of the room a row of slot machines was lined up. A woman was slapping cards on a table in front of some men and women. At another table a man was rolling dice.

Pickle remembered he once went with Pa, when he was feeling good, to a shack on the other side of Lutherville, down a dirt road into the pines. Pa shot craps half the night, it seemed. He gave Pickle a handful of coins for the slot machines. It didn't take long to lose them. Pa won a fistful of bills. "Don't you tell your ma where we been," he warned on the way home, "or I'll tan your hide. I said we was going to look for a coon dog. A coon dog, you understand?"

"You going to get us a dog?" Pickle had asked.

"What do I need a dog for? You and your mother give me enough trouble already," Pa had replied.

Pickle turned to Price, who was drinking his beer from a bottle. "You got a quarter, Price?"

Price reached in his pocket for a quarter. "Your RC's there on the bar."

Pickle carried the bottle over to the slot machines. Some of them took nickels; others, dimes; still others, quarters and half-dollars; and a couple were for silver dollars. He dropped the quarter in a slot and pulled the heavy handle. One bar, two bars, three bars. There was a clanging of coins and a storm of quarters spilled out of the machine onto the floor.

Pickle bent down to pick them up. He stuffed the quarters into his pockets. The woman from the card table came over. "How old are you, kid?"

Without thinking, Pickle answered, "Fourteen."

"You're under age. I'll take the money." She put out a beefy hand.

Price now bent down to help Pickle pick up the last few coins. He handed them to Pickle. "How come it's illegal for the boy here, and it's legal for those folks to shoot craps and play blackjack?" Price asked, pointing to the men and women at the tables. "It looks to me like they're gambling, too. You keep the money, Pickle."

"Hey, Chris, we got a wise guy here," the blond woman called.

The barman left the bar. He held a short club in his hand. "You can keep the money, kid," he said to Pickle. He turned to Price. "We used to have a sign over the door into the bar, Bears and Skunks and Negroes Not Allowed. After a while we took it down. Only the bears could read it. Now, you get on out of here with your beer. Take the kid with you and don't come back." A couple of men came up to stand behind Chris.

"Come on, Pickle, let's hit the road," Price said.

"What about my RC? I left it on the slot machine."

"We'll get another one down the road." Price handed the empty beer bottle to Chris. He walked slowly through the lobby out the door to the street. He leaned against the Dodge and kicked a clod of mud. Pickle took his arm. "There wasn't no point in fighting, Price. There was too many of them. Anyway, we got their money, two pockets full."

"It wasn't that there were too many of them. It was that too many of them were white."

"I would have helped you, Price. You know that. They would have had to beat me, too, and I ain't black."

"That's a good thought, Pickle," Price said. He put his arm around Pickle's shoulders. "You reckon you have enough in your pockets for a tank of gas to get us out of Jackson, Wyoming?"

Pickle jangled the coins. He pulled out a handful. "More than that. Twenty dollars, maybe. Enough to buy gas all the way to California."

A shadow stretched over them. Standing on the steps,

the light from the hotel lobby full in back of him, was a tall broad man. He was weaving back and forth. He took a flat bottle from the pocket of his fringed leather jacket. Carefully, he unscrewed the cap. He put the bottle to his mouth and drank. And drank and drank. He carefully screwed the cap back on the bottle. He held the bottle gently over a rock beside the steps. He let it fall. It flew into pieces. The smell of whiskey seeped down to the road.

The man stepped down. He held his hand out to Price. "How do you do?" he said. "Welcome to the club. I am Sawyer Two Feathers."

16

Price took the hand. "My name is Price Douglas," he said. "This is my friend John Pickel Sherburn. We call him Pickle."

"Ah, the fortunate winner at the slot machine," Sawyer said. "You *were* lucky, Mr. Sherburn. I would wager those machines pay off no more often than once a year. Put it in your pocket tight, boy, where the wolves, the human kind, can't get at it."

Sawyer Two Feathers studied the pickup. "Is this your chariot?" he demanded. He peered down at the license plates. "I note you are not from these parts. You have come to see the snowy breasts of the Grand Tetons?"

The Indian paused. "You do not understand, do you? Tetons, that's what the French called the mountains, Big Breasts. I like that better than the Indian words. That is what they are, indeed, great snowy breasts."

Price was confused. Pickle was bound to be even more confused. He shouldn't be listening to this kind of talk. His ma wouldn't approve, he knew that. There was no telling what this huge, drunken man would say next. Price opened the truck door to get in. He would take Pickle on down the road.

"Ah," Sawyer Two Feathers said, "I observe that you are about to depart. Could I request a ride to my abode?"

"What's he talking about?" Pickle whispered. He had sneaked behind Price into the driving seat. "Does he want a ride?"

"You are clairvoyant, John Sherburn," the Indian boomed. "I do indeed want a ride. It is a long way home for a man on wobbly legs. I will sit up front with you to guide you along the way." Two Feathers eased himself into the seat next to Pickle.

Disgusted, Price climbed into the back. By rights the Indian should be sitting there.

"You may call me Sawyer, that is my father's name, or Two Feathers, the name my mother's people gave me. I am indifferent to names. As you know, friend John, it is the man inside who counts." He unscrewed the cap from a full bottle and tilted it between his lips.

"Let us be off," he instructed. "Turn around here and follow the road until I tell you to turn left. That was an illegal drink, Mr. Sherburn. There is a point of distinction between Mr. Douglas and me. I am not allowed to buy alcohol, Mr. Douglas is not supposed to. A very fine point, mind you, but an important one. The thing is they like the money in the bar more than they like the law, so they sell it to me and I drink it, Mr. Sherburn, and after a while I go to sleep."

Sawyer Two Feathers put his head back and began to snore.

Pickle wondered what he was supposed to do. His shoulders ached from fighting the ruts. He was tired and he was very hungry. He stopped the Dodge and leaned out the door. "He's asleep, Price. Where do I go?"

Price was still disgusted. "Most likely he's passed out. We ought to dump him here beside the road." He swung his leg over to the fender and jumped to the ground. He took a bandanna handkerchief from his pocket. He soaked it in a puddle. "Here, wipe his face with this. Open the window on his side. Tell him to stick his face out."

Pickle did as Price told him. Two Feathers groaned, opened his eyes, and slouched against the door. "Stick your head out the window," Pickle said. "Stick it out and tell me where to go."

"Keep on going up the road. I'll tell you when to turn." He started to snore again.

"Shoot," Pickle muttered. "Some vacation this is." He put the Dodge in gear and started off again.

After half an hour, the snoring ceased. Two Feathers sat up straight. "Turn left at the big white birch tree."

Pickle wrenched the pickup from the ruts onto a rocky road that headed down through some trees and across a wide pasture. The moon had appeared. The outlines of an awesome mountain filled the horizon. The track ended at the shore of a lake that reflected the light of the moon. A dark square shape was framed on the edge of the lake.

Two Feathers awoke again. He pushed the door open. "Thank you. I can make it from here," he laughed. "May we meet again in a happier land in a better time." He staggered to the door of the cabin and kicked it open.

"Wait a minute, darn it," Price called. "You can't leave us here. What are we supposed to do now?"

"Roll on, sweet chariot, roll on." The door shut.

Price climbed into the cab. "What are we going to do, Pickle, drive all night?"

Pickle got out and looked at the moonlit field. "I don't see any bears. I can't go no farther. Driving on that dirt road is a torment. You sleep here, but don't stick your feet out. I'll sleep in back." He dragged his kit bag from under the seat. I've got something here that will take care of the bears, he thought.

Price was too discouraged to argue. The beer and the nasty scene in the hotel bar had exhausted him. Pickle was right. Bears lived in the woods. He shivered. He closed the windows, buttoned up his jacket and rolled up a pair of pants for a pillow. He curled up on the seat and slept.

Pickle stretched out under the canvas. It was damp, but Dr. Plum's mattress was dry. He unzipped the kit bag and laid Pa's pistol on top. Just let Mr. Bear come, he'll be sorry he did, Pickle told himself.

Pickle had never slept harder in his whole life. He was still doubled up on his side when he heard, it seemed, a shout, like when Ma or Pa shouted up the steps in the morning for him to get a move on. Let them shout. He put his arm over his head and went back to sleep.

When he awoke again it was for good. He sat up and looked over the edge of the truck. Now he remembered: Two Feathers, the cabin, the moon reflected on the lake, and the giant shape of the mountains. A blue jay squawked from a pine tree beside the cabin. They got jays here, too, he thought. They sound just the same as the ones at home, always fussing about something.

He stared across the lake at Grand Teton. That's what the ranger called it. It was sure some kind of a mountain, jagged brown-gray rock reaching right up into the clouds. Pickle couldn't be sure, but it looked like patches of snow way up at the top. His gaze moved closer to the lake in front of him. Water rippled around a brown rock close to land. Just then the rock moved. Then it thrashed and shook and stood erect. It was Sawyer Two Feathers, naked as the day he was born.

He strode ashore, a fish clutched in his big hand. The fish struggled and gargled. The Indian seized it with his other hand. He held it up for Pickle to see. "Good morning, Mr. Sherburn. Behold our breakfast, a noble trout."

Sawyer disappeared into his cabin. Pickle climbed to the ground. He went to the open door and looked in. Sawyer was pulling his pants on. The fish was flopping on the floor. "Come in, come in," he called. "You are my guest in this humble abode."

Sawyer pulled his long, black hair back and twisted the water out. He tied it together with a piece of dirty string. He slipped into an old flannel shirt and sat on a hand-made chair to pull his boots on.

There wasn't much for Pickle to see in the cabin: a stone fireplace, charred logs smoking inside, a rough wooden table with a bottle of catsup, some unwashed plates and a coal oil lamp on top, and an unmade bed in the corner. Filling another corner were furs and hides stacked almost as high as Pickle. On the wall over the fireplace, some snowshoes, rifle, and a shotgun.

"And my library, friend John, I don't believe you have observed that." Two Feathers pointed over Price's shoulder toward the door. There, on planks stretching from either side of the door to the wall, books were piled on top of books.

Pickle wasn't much interested in the books. He felt he had to say something to please Sawyer. "That's a lot of books. Do you live here all the time?"

"Oh, yes. I am a permanent resident. They say I am the last live Indian left in Jackson Hole. There are plenty of dead ones here tucked under piles of rocks. Well, what do you think of my residence, Mr. Sherburn? You and your friend, Mr. Douglas, are my first guests here since, let me see . . ." Two Feathers put his finger to his lips and closed his eyes to remember. He opened his eyes and laughed. "My first guests ever. What do you say to that?"

Pickle didn't know what to say. He didn't understand what Two Feathers was talking about half the time. "It must be pretty lonely here in the winter. You mean nobody's ever been here before?" he asked.

"Oh, indeed they have, many people come here: fishermen, campers, surveyors, geologists, miners, rangers, and one time, even the great Senator Phelps himself. A fine upstanding man. A generous man, too. We stood under the pine tree and he told me he owned all this land, but I could stay here a while longer."

"Gosh," Pickle said. He asked Sawyer who Senator Phelps was.

"Senator Phelps? A distinguished American, Mr. Sherburn. His family owned slaves along the Mississippi, I understand, men like Mr. Douglas. Now he owns land. He buys and sells land like his grandfather bought and sold people. I told the senator that my people owned this land. It is ours by treaty with the federal government. I told him that I intended to stay here forever."

"You told him that?"

"I did, but to no avail, I fear. Senator Phelps bought this land of my ancestors from his countrymen who did not own it, and sold most of it to his government. The rangers came down here to tell me it is their land now, that my land is on the other side of the mountains. Reservation land, they call it."

"Price and I have been there. We made a fire beside the river and cooked supper. Have you ever been there?"

"Many times, Mr. Sherburn. I was born there. My mother still lives there with her people. She is a princess."

Pickle wondered if that made Sawyer's father a king or a chief. Maybe Sawyer himself was a chief. What was he doing in those dirty farm clothes, then? "You don't live with your ma and pa?" he asked.

Sawyer shook his head. "I used to live with my mother in Wind River country. It was dry, worthless land, nothing to burn and nothing to hunt. My father was a government agent there, a white man. He went away without my mother. She lives with her people. I will clean the fish for our breakfast. Blow on the coals in the fireplace. You will find potatoes under the table. Lay them in the ashes."

"Yes, sir," said Pickle.

Sawyer turned around. "You call me sir, Mr. Sherburn? Why do you address a poor Indian as sir?"

"That's what Pa said I had to do. I had to say sir to grown-ups, unless they were—"

"Were what, Mr. Sherburn?"

"Negroes," Pickle answered softly.

"And Indians?"

"Pa didn't say about Indians. I ain't never met one before."

"And your friend who is asleep in the truck?"

"That's Price. I just call him Price."

"You are a strange boy, Mr. Sherburn. Let me tell you

that you are the first white person to set foot in my cabin, the very first. Do you know why?"

"No, sir."

"Because of your friend, Mr. Price Douglas. You came with him. He is a member of my club. He is welcome and that makes you welcome. Do you know what club I am talking about, Mr. Sherburn?"

"No, sir."

"It has many names, the Black and Brown Club, the Outcasts' Club, the Unwhite Club, take your choice. Do you understand, Mr. Sherburn? I am sorry that you cannot be a member, but you may certainly be a guest. Is that all right with you?"

"I guess so. What do I call you, sir?"

"Anything you want to, John Pickel Sherburn. Indians do not use titles. Now, you start on the fire."

‖ 17 ‖

The smell of the fish cooking over the open fire drifted from the cabin. It floated through the holes in the truck to Price's nostrils. The sunlight was warming the cab. Price roused himself. He looked through the cab window. Where was Pickle? Price rolled down the window. "Pickle!" he shouted.

"I'm coming," Pickle shouted back from the doorway. "I have to pull the potatoes out of the fire. You go wash the sleep out of your eyes."

Pickle hurried inside. He took the pointed stick from the hearth that Two Feathers said was for the potatoes. He poked it into one. Steam shot out. They were done. He took the other two out and put them on the table.

Two Feathers bent over the fish cooking on the coals in some sort of wire contraption. "It's done, too, Mr. Sherburn. Bring your friend in."

Pickle found Price kneeling on the sand, rinsing his face. "Ain't it something, Price? Did you ever see anything like this? I sure never did. I washed Sawyer's plates here with sand. The egg comes right off. It's time to eat, Price. I cooked the potatoes in the fireplace."

Price followed the boy into the cabin. Two handmade

chairs were set at the table. Sawyer Two Feathers had turned a fat log on its end and sat waiting at the table. "Good morning, Mr. Douglas," he greeted Price. "Friend John and I have prepared breakfast." He took a wicked-looking knife from the sheath on his belt and cut the fish into three pieces. He put a piece on each plate. Pickle added a slightly charred potato.

Price took a bite of fish. Sometimes at the work camp the cook made a rotten fish stew with tomatoes and rice and anything else he had. The men generally pushed it away. But Sawyer's fish was delicious. He finished it before he started on his burnt potato. He couldn't hurt Pickle's feelings. He noticed that Pickle and Two Feathers were eating their potatoes like an apple. He did the same. The crisp burned skin tasted good. This was the way to go camping, he decided.

Pickle gathered up the three plates. "I'll be right back," he announced. "Don't make no plans without me, hear?"

He took the plates and forks to the lake. He scoured them with sand. Little silverfish darted toward him to snatch crumbs. The sun was halfway high now. The mountain stood behind the lake in massive magnificence. Ain't that something? Pickle thought. Won't I have something to tell Pa? He bet his father had never seen a mountain like Grand Teton. It was really something.

"Two Feathers says you can go with him, if you want to," Price told Pickle.

"Where's he going?" Pickle asked.

"To procure supplies, Mr. Sherburn. We have eaten the last potato. I have nothing left for my guests but dried venison. I doubt that it will be agreeable to your tastes."

"I'll get the truck started. We ought to buy ourselves a tent and some blankets, don't you think, Price, if we are going to stay here for a while?"

"There is no need for that, friend John. You already have the warmest beds you will ever find." Sawyer motioned to the pile of hides. "All we need is our daily bread, our 'grub' as the ranchers call it."

"Okay," Pickle said, "but we'll buy, won't we, Price? We haven't spent much of our money."

"The supplies do not cost money," Sawyer Two Feathers explained, "and we will not need your truck. We will use other means of travel."

"Huh?"

"You will find a canoe at the back of the cabin. It is, alas, a white man's canoe, but superior, I am obliged to admit, to those made by my ancestors. See if you can drag it to the water."

A canoe trip, that would really be something. Pickle ran around to the back of the cabin. A silver canoe leaned against the log wall. Pickle eased it to the ground. Why, it seemed as light as a feather. He bent over to lift it. Sideways, he carried it to the shore. He returned for the three paddles.

"Two paddles will be a sufficiency, Mr. Sherburn," Sawyer told him when he came to the canoe with some gunnysacks over his shoulder.

"What about Price? Ain't he going?"

"Perhaps the next time. I believe Mr. Douglas wants to sit under a pine tree and contemplate the grandeur of my country. And," Two Feathers went on, "we need the middle space in the canoe for our provisions. It is a long trip. Get in, friend John, and I will shove off."

The Indian took a paddle and began to propel the silver canoe along the shore, his long, powerful strokes driving the paddle deep into the water. He swept the paddle from one side to another. Pickle turned on his narrow seat to face ahead. A gentle breeze folded around him. He trailed his hand in the water for a moment to feel the movement of the canoe.

Shoot, he thought, what do I have to go to California for? He wondered if Sawyer Two Feathers would let him stay with him for a couple of years until he was old enough for his driving license and went out on the road with his rig. He could come back and stay at the cabin when he wasn't on the road. He would write Ma and Pa a letter saying he was all right and would stay in touch.

And Price? He couldn't let Price have the Dodge; he and Sawyer would need that. He would take Price to the bus depot and he could go home to Detroit with all the money they had. Sawyer didn't seem to need any money. He said he got his grub free.

Or, better still, maybe Price would stay on. He could postpone going to college for a year or two. When he thought about it real hard, Pickle couldn't see himself getting along without Price. He needed Price, and he half suspected Price needed him. Both of them were strangers out here in this unknown country, and for all Pickle knew, the law was still after them. Maybe he could talk Price into staying on until the snows came. Then they would leave. They could go to California later.

Pickle was startled from his reverie by Sawyer's deep voice. "A penny for your thoughts, friend John."

"I dunno. I was just thinking about how nice it was here and maybe I'd like to live here someday."

"This *is* the land of dreams, you are right. It was sacred land to my people and other Indian peoples, too. It was their hunting ground. It was filled with buffalo and deer and wild sheep and food from the ground and the lake. Some of them lived here; others returned in winter to their homes on the plains."

Sawyer stopped paddling. The canoe drifted in a wide turn toward the shore. The Indian put the paddle in the water to turn it straight. "It is still a land of dreams, Mr. Sherburn. My people dream of a land that was theirs. They sit on their land in the thirsty reservation and fight and drink and drink and dream. The white men like Senator Phelps who have taken the land dream of gold and cattle and lumber and fortunes to be made. They want to hold time still, but time is like the water of the lake."

Sawyer reached over the side of the canoe. He cupped his hand and held it out for Pickle to see. The water trickled from his hand into the lake. "You can't hold time any more than you can hold water in your hand, friend John. What was, only our fathers know. What is, only the white man knows. What will be, only the great god knows. Keep dreaming, Mr. Sherburn, and I will keep paddling."

"Where are we going?" Pickle asked. "Where is the store at?"

"You must be patient in this life. All will be revealed to you in good time. I will tell you when we arrive. Then you will know. Afterward, you will forget. Keep dreaming, Mr. Sherburn."

Toward sunset, Pickle perceived the shape of a house in the distance. Smoke was trailing into the sky above it. As the canoe drew closer, the house became bigger— and bigger. A road wound down from the trees at the top of the slope across the field. Now he could see other smaller buildings clustered around the huge ranch house. In the field between the house and the lake stood a stretch of corn and what seemed to be a garden and a livestock pen.

"Is that the store yonder?" he called to Two Feathers.

Sawyer put his finger to his lips. He held up the palm of his hand for Pickle to be quiet. He turned the canoe toward a rocky beach where a cluster of trees stood between them and the houses. He reached out his hand to help Pickle to the land. He placed his paddle carefully in the bottom of the canoe, which he pulled halfway out of the water. He took from his pocket a piece of dried meat. He cut off a section and held it out to Pickle. "It is all I have to offer you, Mr. Sherburn," he said.

Pickle tore at the meat with his teeth. It was tough. And it smelled bad, like an old ham Pa kept hanging too long in the garage. He stopped chewing. Should he spit it out? That didn't seem right. He reckoned he better swallow it down and not try to chew on it anymore. Pickle forced the wad of venison down his throat. He gagged. Tears came to his eyes.

Sawyer Two Feathers did not laugh. "You are a brave boy and a loyal guest, friend John. You accept the inevitable. That is good. It is how we must live our lives. The inevitable is never very far away."

"How come we're waiting here?" Pickle asked. He swatted a horde of mosquitoes away from his face. "The store will be closed pretty soon."

"That is what I am waiting for, friend John, for Senator Phelps to close his store."

"That's the senator's store?" Pickle asked. Pickle did not really understand. You couldn't go after the store was closed. Was Two Feathers going to rob the store?

"You mean you came to steal some of his stuff?" he brought himself to ask.

"Not precisely, Mr. Sherburn. I regard it as more of a barter. We are exchanging. Senator Phelps has stolen my land, and I am borrowing some of his food. I was pretty sure that Mr. Douglas would not approve of the arrangement."

"You're right. Price was in jail for three years. He has to be careful. He says he's already a two-time loser."

"And I am a one-time loser. Well, get your gunnysack. Let us go see what Senator Phelps has to offer. Keep low to the ground, if you will. And come quietly. Let us hope he has left a piglet outside. I am rather partial to pork." They made their way up to the cornfield. Two Feathers began stripping the ears from the brown stalks. "This is last year's corn. We will have to steam it, Mr. Sherburn," he whispered. "Help yourself."

From the garden next to the field Two Feathers crept into a storehouse. He filled a bag with dried beans, potatoes, squash, cabbages, and withered apples. He crept up to a pen. He shook his head sadly. "We will have to be vegetarians. Come, we must go. Senator Phelps is a cautious man. He has men with guns to protect his property."

The bag of corn was heavy. Pickle stumbled over the uneven terrain. Two Feathers had two bags slung over his shoulder, which he held with one hand. Pickle came first to the canoe. He started to drop his gunnysack inside. There was no room! The bottom of the canoe was filled with clean white flour bags, newly tied at the top. One of the bags was moving. Pickle heard a squeal.

Sawyer Two Feathers stood beside him. He put his arm around Pickle's shoulders. "Senator Phelps is a mean-hearted man, Mr. Sherburn. He has stolen my land, and now he is stealing my dignity."

"What's he doing this for?" Pickle asked. "We didn't have to go to all the trouble, did we?"

"He wants to show us," Sawyer answered, "that he is rich and we are poor. He sent his men to fill our canoe. He wants to tell me I am a thieving Indian, and he will not accept my barter."

"He got you a pig anyway," Pickle observed.

"Indeed he did. The senator is a religious man. He believes in charity. It is his duty to look after the poor when he has taken their riches. Well, there is no help for it now. We all must eat. Let us find a place for what we have borrowed."

They loaded the canoe. It barely floated above the surface of the water when they took their places. "Do not move too quickly, friend John, or you and I and the pig will be lost."

The Indian leaned back slightly. He handed Pickle the paddle. "I would be obliged if you would take us to our cabin, John. Just follow the shoreline. I must bury my shame."

Two Feathers reached into his jacket pocket. He took out a flat bottle. He unscrewed the cap, which he put back into his pocket. He held the bottle to his lips until it was empty. He dropped it into the lake. He put his elbows on the gunwales and leaned slowly back against the prow. He lifted his head toward the night sky. He closed his eyes and was silent.

|| 18 ||

Pickle heaved a corncob into the lake and shucked another steaming ear. Two Feathers rose to his feet and waded into the water to retrieve the cob. He brought it ashore and placed it beside the fire.

"We must be good to the water that is good to us, John."

The rebuke made Pickle turn red. He remembered the bottle Sawyer dropped into the lake. He started to remind Sawyer, but thought better of it.

Sawyer read his thoughts. "You are remembering last night's bottle, are you not, John? That was a ceremony. No more white man's water. I was telling the lake that I would drink only from its waters henceforth."

Price listened. What were Pickle and Two Feathers talking about? He had been long asleep when they arrived. It had seemed like it was close to dawn, but he couldn't be sure. He had burrowed beneath some of the skins he had taken from the pile and gone to sleep again. He awoke when the sun was high. Pickle was snoring on the mattress at the other end of the room. Two Feathers was kneeling at the fireplace. Dirty gunnysacks and clean, white cloth sacks were piled on the floor next to the table. Outside, Price could swear he heard a pig squealing.

The Indian had stood up and motioned for Price to follow him outside.

"We should not awaken the boy. Your friend, Mr. Douglas, is a strong, resourceful young man. You are proud of him, are you not?"

"I guess so," Price said, not understanding what Pickle had done that was so important.

"You saw our supplies? John helped me obtain them and bring them back. A heavy load for the young man."

"It looks like a lot," Price agreed.

"It is, indeed. We will eat well for a good while. But they were not the test of his manhood, Mr. Douglas. I felt a necessity, you might say, to commemorate the outing, much as I did the other evening when we first met. Friend John brought me home then and brought me home last night. A long distance in the dark with a heavy load and no guide, but John accomplished the task."

Price was astonished. "You mean he rowed—paddled—the canoe all the way back? It must have taken him all night."

"I believe it did. And not a word of complaint. I think your friend must be an Indian, Mr. Douglas. So we must allow him to rest. I will prepare us a meal outside."

Sawyer had dug a hole in the ground and lined it with flat rocks from the shore. He brought some coals from the fireplace and laid pine needles on top. He blew until a flame flared up. Then he added pine cones and dry twigs. When the fire was burning well, he added larger sticks and several logs. When Pickle staggered out of the cabin at noon, Sawyer placed damp ears of dried corn and two hard squash in the ashes. He brought a trout ashore he had been keeping with a string through its mouth.

Now they sat around the fire after the meal, full and lazy. "You paddled the boat all night, Pickle?" Price asked. "Are you sure Two Feathers didn't help you?"

"I did," Pickle answered. "It wasn't no worse than driving the Dodge in the ruts all day."

"And you helped with all those bags and the pig out back?" Price went on.

Pickle looked across the fire at Two Feathers, who had his face down.

"Yes," he replied.

"Where did you get those flour sacks?" Price asked, his suspicions now aroused. "You didn't take those with you."

"They were a gift, Mr. Douglas," Sawyer spoke up. "There is a generous man who lives far down the shore who likes to help poor people."

"What you are saying is that you stole the stuff, is that what you mean?" Price accused Two Feathers. He shook his head. "That boy's in enough trouble. Maybe me, too. Tell him about the truck, Pickle."

"I took the truck from my pa," Pickle admitted.

"You mean the county, don't you, Pickle?"

"Yeah, the county," the boy whispered.

"I am confident he had good reasons. John Pickle is an honest man. He would only take what he needed. That is not stealing, Mr. Douglas. John will give it back in other ways in another time."

"That's not what the juvenile judge said when he sent me to the reformatory," Price remarked. "He said taking candy bars and fruit and soda pop and money was stealing."

"That was a white man's opinion, Mr. Douglas."

The judge certainly hadn't been black, Pickle remembered. He was a fat, gray-haired man with cold blue eyes behind his glasses. When the social worker tried to explain that Price was young and behaving like other kids on the street and she would accept responsibility for his behavior from now on, the judge told her to be quiet. "I have heard all that before," he said, and sentenced Price to a year in the reformatory.

"It was a white man's opinion when they caught me riding in a car my cousin Clarence had stolen. Two years in Pickle's pa's work camp that cost me. I reckon I have to live by white man's opinions, whether I want to or not. I don't have a cabin by the lake and rich friends who don't care if I steal from them," Price said resentfully.

Two Feathers put the fish bones and cobs and squash skins on top of the fire. They began to smoke. He stirred them around with his pointed stick.

"It's not my cabin, Mr. Douglas, and you are already aware it's not my land. It's the government's. You and your friend are traveling in a stolen truck, you tell me. I have been living in a stolen—or borrowed—cabin on somebody else's land. Our fates coincide, Mr. Douglas."

"You mean it ain't—isn't—your cabin?" Pickle asked. "Who's it belong to?"

"No one now, I suppose, but probably to the government since it sits on their land. Years ago when I graduated from the university, I came here. I was too civilized, they said, to live on the reservation. They meant I might cause trouble. I returned to the land of my fathers. I found this shack beside the lake. No one seemed to care;

I moved in and fixed it up. I became a hunter. I sold the skins for what I needed."

"Gosh," Pickle said, "You must be rich, with all the furs you have."

"Life is filled with complexities, John. Some of those skins I cannot sell because they belonged to animals I was not supposed to shoot. The government protects them. It protects those animals better than it protects its people, at least my people. I think I shot them to teach the animals they weren't any better than a poor Indian."

Price thought he was better off than Sawyer Two Feathers, no matter what happened to him. He felt a great sorrow for the man. He watched him reach into his pocket and withdraw his hand empty. He needs his bottle, Price realized.

Two Feathers shrugged. He smiled at Pickle. "I made my vow last night to the lake. Now I must keep it, mustn't I?" He stared into the fire and poked it once more.

"After I had been here for a while," he continued, "a policeman from Jackson came across the field in his truck—much like yours—to see what I was up to. He wanted to search my cabin. He did not ask me. He told me. I said he could not, that it was mine. He pushed me out of the way to go inside.

"I made a mistake. I responded violently. While he was unconscious, I burned my hides in the fireplace. Then I put the policeman in the back of his truck and drove him to town. I left it in front of the station and walked home.

"They came back the next day, of course. They came with men and guns and tied me up like a wild calf and sent me to the penitentiary. I served my time and returned. We are quits now, the law and I. If I shoot an illegal animal it is only to prove my independence. But I will not be foolish enough to sell it."

"You've been to the university?" Price asked. "Is that why you talk so fancy? I didn't know what to tell Pickle when he asked."

"I talk this way, Mr. Douglas, because it is how I talk to myself. I have no one else to talk to. I read my books, and I like the fancy words they use, so I use them for myself."

"We stayed with a professor in Madison who knew everything about words," Pickle said. "He could tell exactly where you came from. He had this map on his wall, like one of Price's road maps, only lots bigger, and he'd go right up to the map and put his finger on a place and, sure enough, that was where you come from."

"'Came from,' Mr. Sherburn."

"'Came from.' That's what I meant to say. But I don't think Professor Plum could tell about Two Feathers, do you, Price?"

Price wasn't really listening. How come, he asked himself, this Indian had been to the university, and how come it hadn't done him any good? He ended up in jail just like Price. Maybe a college education didn't make that much difference. So far he had met only two people who had studied at the university, Dr. Plum and Sawyer Two Feathers, and both of them seemed a little crazy to Price. He sure didn't want to end up like either of them.

"Did your mother send you to the university?" he asked. "Did she have some money for you to go?"

"My poor mother never heard of a university, and she didn't have two pennies to rub against each other. Nothing like that. Indians on a reservation didn't worry about education, Mr. Douglas. No, it was the Indian Affairs agent who saw to it that I attended. That was because he found out that I could play football. I received what they called an athletic scholarship. It was a kind of trade. I played football for them and they let me go to classes. I enjoyed a brief fame as a football player. I could run with the football and I played barefoot, the way I did at the Indian school. I was known as the Barefoot Buck, sometimes as the Barefoot Back. It depended on who was talking."

What Sawyer said wasn't going to do Price much good. He didn't even play on the Sunday softball team the men at the camp had. "Could you have gone without playing football?" he wanted to know.

"I cannot say. I was given entrance because I could run with a football. After a year, I decided I wasn't going to be a barefoot Indian anymore. I was a foolish example to my people. One day I put the ball down at the coach's feet and walked away. In turn, they took away my scholarship. But I liked it there, Mr. Douglas, and I stayed. I found a job that suited me: putting books on the shelves of the university library. That was the beginning of my education. It is why I talk fancy, as friend John here says. In the library I found out who I was. That is where I began to dream."

Price recalled that his mother was always after Franklin and him to get some education so they could move up in the world. She didn't say anything about learning who you were and how to dream. "Didn't you want to get ahead?" he asked Sawyer. "Didn't you want to be a lawyer or a doctor or somebody important? I don't know yet what I am going to be, but I sure know that I'm not going to be what I have been up to now. I have one more year of school. Then I'm going to the university, too."

"Price is teaching me," Pickle said. "I do my books while Price drives the truck. I'm almost through my fifthgrade lessons. I won't be too far behind if I decide to go back home."

"*When* you go back home," Price corrected him.

"I see," Two Feathers said. He wasn't really listening. He had a faraway look in his dark eyes. He pushed the corncobs under the ashes with the pointed stick. He took his straw hat to the lake and filled it with water. He spilled the water on the remains of the fire. It hissed and sent up a puff of steam.

Two Feathers stood beside the fire. "At the library they gave me the discarded books and the duplicates. I filled boxes with them, and when I had finished at the university and they gave me a piece of paper they called a diploma, I came home to the reservation. There was no room for the boxes in my mother's hut. There was no light at night to read them by. They did not want me to teach at the Indian school. They were afraid I would teach things the students were not supposed to know. I had nothing to say to my brothers, and they had nothing to say to me. I don't believe I was meant to be anyone else. Now I cannot be anyone else. I already am."

Sawyer Two Feathers turned away. He walked into his cabin and shut the door.

Something was wrong. Pickle could feel that something wrong. It was like when Pa and Ma had a really big fight in the kitchen, Ma screaming at Pa because he never paid her any mind and Pa shouting back that she wasn't any good, always at Vinnie's, and the house was a mess. Myrna would slip into Pickle's room and sit on the bed and look scared. The shouting would stop after a while, sometimes when Pa would give Ma a slap across the face and storm out the door to the pickup to go over to the bunkhouse. In the silence everything stopped—just like now—and you waited for sound to fill the silence to tell you it was all right again. Maybe Myrna would take his hand and rub the back of it to let Pickle know she was still there. They sat there together, not really wanting to because deep down Myrna didn't like Pickle and he sure didn't think much of his sister, but in the silence they needed each other.

Price was a grown-up, Pickle reckoned, and Two Feathers, too, but they acted like him half the time, maybe Sawyer less than Price, but they were both grown-ups. He could see that things weren't going all that well with either of them, Price with his ma dead and the street gangs waiting for him, and Two Feathers alone here in his cabin away from his people who didn't want him, drinking whiskey and reading his books.

And he was left with the silence. Shoot, he thought, there wasn't any point in sitting here until it got dark and the mosquitos started in on them. "Hey, Price," he said, "what do you say to a swim in the lake?"

"Why not?" Price said. He held out his hand. "Give me a pull up. I'm stiff from all this sitting around."

‖ 19 ‖

During the days that followed, Sawyer sat under the pine tree reading; at nights he hunched over his book beside the coal oil lamp on the table. He told Pickle and Price to help themselves to anything they wanted: food, canoe, hides, whatever. He ate very little, a strip of venison or a handful of beans. Several times he arose, stretched his giant arms, and went to drink from the lake.

"Forgive me," he responded to Pickle when the boy asked him if he was all right, "if I am ungracious to my guests. There are times when I must flee from myself into my books. Now is such a time. It will pass, Mr. Sherburn, it will pass."

"Leave him be, Pickle," Price said. "I think he's missing his whiskey. Or maybe something worse is wrong. He sure is a strange man. I can't figure him out."

"Did we do anything?" Pickle asked uneasily. He hoped it would pass pretty soon. Two Feathers had promised to take them across the lake to Grand Teton.

"I don't think so," Price said. "You better feed the little pig. I haven't got the heart to kill him."

"I've already been feeding him. Pigs are smart. He's

rooting around for himself. Maybe Two Feathers will keep him for a friend."

One day they drove down to Jackson for coffee and gasoline. Price asked Sawyer if he wanted to go. Without a word the Indian climbed into the back of the truck. When Price and Pickle came out of the store with the coffee and some candy bars and soft drinks, Sawyer was seated in back of the truck as though he had never moved, but he held a paper bag in his lap. Price offered him a bottle of RC Cola. Sawyer shook his head.

"We got to take a look at that mountain before we go to California, Price. How long do you reckon it will take us to get to the top? It looks like an all-day hike. I'm going to ask Two Feathers. He must have climbed up there lots of times."

Sawyer was leaning against his pine tree, straw hat tipped over his face. At the end of the tether, the pig was sleeping close to Sawyer's feet. It scrambled up and squealed as Pickle came close.

"You awake, Sawyer?" Pickle asked.

Two Feathers pushed his hat back. "I am deep in my thoughts, friend John, but I am awake."

"I keep looking over the lake at that mountain, Grand Teton or whatever. I've been wanting to get to the top ever since I saw it. It would be something to tell Pa, that I got to the top of a mountain that went three miles up into the air."

"Sit down, John," Two Feathers said. "You must understand that some mountains are to climb and others are to see. Grand Teton is to see."

"Darn! You mean I can't go over there in a canoe and walk up the side?"

Sawyer smiled, the first time Pickle had seen him smile in days. "The mountain is a long way from here, friend John. It only looks close because it is so big and the air is so clear. From here it looks as though you can walk up the sides, but that is not so. Men use ropes and clamps and cleated boots and all the other things men use to climb mountains. Sometimes when the god of the mountain is angry with them he gives a little shrug and they fall to the bottom. Other times he doesn't care. He lets them stomp in his snows and take his picture."

Two Feathers saw the boy's disappointment. "We cannot climb the mountain. We are not supposed to, because it is forbidden to my people and to you and Mr. Douglas because you are my guests. But we can visit. We will pay our respects to the mountain, and I will ask the god to make my troubles go away."

"What troubles?" Pickle demanded. "It looks to me like Price and I have all the troubles. If I go home, my pa will beat me until I can't sit down and send me back to school. Price has some tough guys waiting for him out on the street, and for all I know, the police are looking after both of us for stealing the county's truck."

Sawyer stood up and put his hat on straight. "I will ask the god of the mountain to make your troubles go away, too."

Before dawn the next morning, Price, Pickle, and Sawyer Two Feathers set off across the lake with their bedding and a flour sack of provisions. Pickle in the bow and Sawyer in the stern drove the silver canoe through the water. Price sat huddled in the middle, feeling useless.

"Do not despair, Mr. Douglas," Two Feathers said. "In a while you and Mr. Sherburn will trade places, if you wish. I have put a book in the sack to help you pass the time. It was written by one of my ancestors."

Price reached into his sack to draw out a tattered book that looked a hundred years old. The yellowed pages were loose; some of the faded photographs fell into his lap. He tucked them back in as best he could after looking at them. They were pictures of stern-faced Indians standing beside their tents or their horses, some of them in feathered headdress. There were little Indian children bundled up and tied into some kind of shed. Price turned to the first pages. The book was *History of the Shoshone,* by Albert Cloudwatcher. The author's picture showed him to be a big, grim Indian in a black suit with no tie and a white felt hat set squarely on his head.

"Cloudwatcher was a preacher for a while," Two Feathers called to Price. "He went to mission school and became a preacher and wrote a book. After that, he became what he was before."

Price wasn't sure what Albert Cloudwatcher had been to start with. He tried to make himself comfortable while he read about Sawyer's people.

Pickle stumbled over the rocky terrain. "Where does the mountain begin?" he asked impatiently. "I don't know how long we've been walking, and it ain't no closer."

"'Isn't any closer,' John. Unless you talk properly, Mr. Douglas will feel that he has failed as a teacher. You are almost there; look behind you."

Pickle turned around. Two Feathers was right. The lake and the canoe, like a speck on the beach, were lying well below them. The sun had disappeared. They were climbing now in shadows.

"You said we hadn't ought to climb the mountain, the god wouldn't like it."

"So I did, John. I have not forgotten. We are only crawling between the mountain's toes. This is where we will stay." He pointed ahead of them. "Do you see that flat ledge ahead of us? It is a protected place that campers use where rocks will not fall on us."

Pickle remembered what the ranger had said about bears. He asked Two Feathers.

"Not this time of year. Later, yes. Tonight we will be all right outside."

Under an overhang, Sawyer kicked away charcoal logs and debris. "Wrap yourselves warmly," he told Pickle and Price. "It will get cold very quickly. I will sleep now." He pulled a blanket around him and curled up on his side.

Price and Pickle crept out on the ledge with candy bars and colas. It was dark now. The rocks that had been warm to the touch were chill as they sat beneath the mountain.

"Is Two Feathers right about the god of the mountain? Where do you think he lives?" Pickle asked.

"Didn't you go to Sunday School, Pickle?" Price asked. He could remember that on Sundays his mother stuffed Franklin and him into starched white shirts and they marched, Ma and Ruth in front, the boys straggling behind, to a storefront church where the preacher had shaken the Bible at them and told them they were going to Hell if they didn't behave. They sang some songs, and after the service ran home to the streets to do everything the preacher cautioned them not to do.

"Nah," Pickle said. Ma and Pa hadn't held much with going to church.

"Well, Sawyer's people believe in different things from you and me," Price explained. "I was reading that old book in the canoe. They think that there is a great spirit, some kind of a god, that lives in the mountain here. He doesn't have a place. He's just there. Can't you feel something sort of different out here in the dark with that mountain looking down on you and stars piled on top of stars over your head?"

Pickle unwrapped a candy bar. He shook his head. Realizing that Price couldn't see him, he spoke, his mouth full of caramel and chocolate and peanuts. "No."

"What?" Price asked.

"No," Pickle almost shouted.

"Well, I do, and you ought to, too, Pickle. You'd be better off growing up believing in something besides an old Dodge truck."

"It's got us this far, Price. When it stops, maybe I'll believe in something else."

Price was getting cold. There was no point in trying to educate Pickle about things he wasn't sure of himself. "I'm going to my fur bed. You coming?"

"I reckon," Pickle replied. "There's nothing else to do out here."

Three hikers crossed the ledge at dawn. Price sat up, frightened. They waved happily and disappeared behind the rocks. The sun began to rise beyond the trees across the lake. Price had never been so conscious of his smallness. I'm just a speck here on a rock, he thought, that nobody knows about or cares about, except maybe Pickle.

Two Feathers stood in back of him. "It is a considerable sight, is it not, Mr. Douglas? I'll wager you are thinking how unimportant you are."

Price nodded. "I haven't ever seen anything like it. It's so big and empty."

"Once there were tents and horses and my people out there, Mr. Douglas. It was not always empty. Soon there will be Senator Phelps's people there. You have seen them already this morning, I believe, in their shorts and knapsacks and boots, going somewhere on the mountain."

"Who?" said Pickle. "I didn't see nobody." He shivered.

"Come, Mr. Sherburn, stretch your limbs. We have a journey to make. I think I would like one of your soft drinks for breakfast and a bar of chocolate, if you can spare it."

"Where are we going?" Pickle asked.

"Why do you want to know everything in advance, John? You must leave room for surprises in your life. Let us say we are going in search of bats."

Two Feathers led them around the base of Grand Teton. It seemed to Price they doubled and turned among the rocks and trees and bushes for hours. Finally they slipped between the narrow walls of a crevice. Two Feathers bent down to examine the dirt and pebbles between their feet.

"What are you looking for, gold?" Pickle wanted to know. "Is this a gold mountain?"

Sawyer shook his head. "It is not, friend John. I am looking to see if the pebbles I arranged when I was here last year have been disturbed. They will tell me if someone has passed this way."

The walls of the little canyon forced them to walk sideways. They came to a low, jagged hole. "We must go in on our bellies," Two Feathers said. "Follow me. Do not be frightened."

A patch of sunlight on the sand beyond the hole told Pickle and Price they were inside a cave. They heard a chittering and scuffling overhead. Two Feathers struck a match. He lit a knotted branch, which flared into a steady flame. There was a whirring and the air was filled with bats, which darted and dived and retreated deeper into the cave. Price felt that he was going to be sick.

Two Feathers swept the flaming pine branch around the cave. "Behold the armory of the Shoshone."

Lined against the walls were rifles and spears and sagging bows and clutches of arrows tied together. Sawyer picked a long feathered headdress from the floor. "A war bonnet, the white soldiers called it. There are a hundred of them here waiting for the Indian horsemen who will never come."

The pitch pine burned close to Sawyer's head. He lit another. "Did you read of my people's last stand?" he asked Price.

Price shook his head. "I only looked at the pictures and read the first pages."

"A long time ago—eighty years, to be exact—when the white farmers and hunters began to steal our land, my ancestors, who were peaceful people, determined to defend themselves. Secretly they prepared to attack the whites. They collected a few rifles and made their spears and arrows. They stored them here to be ready for the day of the attack.

"But that day never arrived. One of my drunken ancestors betrayed his people to the soldiers. They attacked the villages across the lake one morning. They shot the young men and drove the rest of my people away. Now the bats and I are the keepers of the armory. You will not reveal my secret?" Sawyer Two Feathers said finally. "Who can tell? The day may yet come when my people will rise up."

The second branch burned low. Two Feathers dropped it on the ground. He motioned for Price and Pickle to crawl out the hole. Carefully, he followed, smoothing the sand and pebbles behind him.

A harsh knock at the door echoed through the cabin the next morning. "I'll go," Pickle mumbled. His canvas bed was closest to the door. He opened it. The ranger from the station stood outside. He recognized Pickle.

"You found a place with Sawyer, did you?" he remarked. "I thought that was your truck outside. You're lucky. Sawyer isn't always that hospitable to campers. Is he in?"

"I'm here, Mr. Marlow," Two Feathers called.

"You weren't here yesterday when I rode down," the ranger said.

"No," Sawyer agreed.

"I was to give you this. It came from park headquarters." He held out an envelope for Sawyer to take.

"Yes." Sawyer took the envelope.

"I've done my job," Marlow said. "I didn't like it, but I did it." He offered his hand to Pickle, who shook it, and to Sawyer Two Feathers, who did not. Marlow shrugged and went out to his horse waiting alongside the Dodge. He waved to Pickle and ambled up the track.

The envelope lay unopened on the table. Price had filled the coffeepot at the lake and placed it on the coals.

When it had percolated he took it to the table. Sawyer drank the bitter coffee and stared at the envelope.

"Aren't you going to read your letter?" Pickle asked. "The ranger brought it all the way down from the station. It must be important."

Sawyer stared at Pickle from a great distance. At last he spoke. "Perhaps, friend John, you and Mr. Douglas would care to make a canoe trip this morning. I must attend to my affairs here."

After that, he had practically shoved Pickle and him out the door, Price thought. He pulled on the paddle and wondered what was wrong. What, in fact, had been wrong since the day Pickle and Two Feathers had stolen the vegetables? Price was no longer comfortable in the cabin. And it was clear that Pickle was confused by the Indian's moodiness. It was time for them to move on.

"What are you thinking, Pickle?" he asked. The boy hadn't said two words since Price had hurried him down to the lake and handed him a paddle.

"I dunno. I have a bad feeling that something is going to happen, a thunderstorm or something. Remember that storm on the way up to Jackson Hole? I was scared then. We didn't have anyplace to go."

"You were in the truck, Pickle. You were safe."

"I guess so, but I was glad I was with you. Sawyer, you know, he doesn't have anybody. I feel sorry for him."

The sound of distant shots echoed across the lake. Startled, Pickle and Price leaned straight to listen.

"They came from back thataway," Pickle said. "Back at the cabin."

"I reckon he shot the little pig," Price said.

"He only needed one shot. That's all they used back

home, even for a big old hog. We better turn around and start paddling, Price."

Another round of shots rattled across the lake. As the canoe rounded a bend in the shore, the cabin stood in view. Two Feathers was throwing things out of the cabin. "Shoot," Pickle exclaimed. "That looks like your suitcase—and the canvas. What's he up to? He could have asked us polite to leave."

Next, Sawyer ran out crazily, shaking an ax over his head.

"He's going to kill the pig, Price."

"He's drunk," Price said.

They watched as Two Feathers raised the ax high. He brought it down on the pig's tether. The pig scrambled into the bushes. Sawyer threw the ax into the lake and lurched back into the cabin.

"We'd better go . . . ," Pickle said.

"We'd better stay right where we are," Price said.

Smoke poured from the cabin, not from the chimney, but the door. Flames licked around the frame. Sawyer emerged. He ripped his flannel shirt off and threw inside. He lifted a bottle to his mouth.

He turned toward the lake. He waved his arms to Price and Pickle. He bent over and picked up his two guns. He took them to the lake; swinging them by the barrel he flung them far out into the water. He shouted something.

"What did he say?" Price said.

Pickle stood up carefully in the bow.

"What?" he shouted to Sawyer.

The Indian's voice came back, "Good-bye, thank you."

"What's he talking about—'good-bye'? Where's he going?" Pickle asked.

Half-naked, Sawyer Two Feathers staggered to the pickup. Pickle and Price saw the door shut. They heard the door slam. They heard the motor coughing.

"It's damp," Pickle said. "Come on, Price, paddle! It won't start right away."

They paddled with all their strength. The sounds of the motor grew weaker.

"Durn fool," Pickle said. "He's running the battery down."

As the silver canoe touched shore, the motor sputtered and caught. It roared as Sawyer gave it gas. It weaved from side to side up the track. A hand shot out the window, waving.

"Stop, you damn fool Indian," Price shouted. "That's *our* truck." He chased after the Dodge.

"Let him go, Price. He ain't stealing it. He'll come back for sure."

The cabin was in full blaze. Pickle gathered up his kit bag. The revolver was still inside. He folded up the canvas and put it with his bag and Price's suitcase away from the heat. He picked up the empty whiskey bottles and put them back in their paper bag. Maybe Two Feathers would want to drown them when he sobered up. A piece of paper fluttered under his feet. Pickle reached for it. With difficulty, he read, "The Department of Interior regrets to inform you that it has been obliged to condemn the property you occupy and requests you under penalty of law to evacuate said property within a period of fifteen days of receipt of this notice." Some other stuff followed that Pickle didn't understand. He let the paper float to the ground.

"There sure was something wrong," he said to himself.

Price appeared on the edge of the woods. He waved his arms. "Bring our stuff up," he shouted.

Pickle gathered up the bags and the canvas. He trudged up to where Price was waiting and followed him to the park road. The Dodge had pushed into the white birch tree and stalled. Sawyer Two Feathers was slumped over the wheel. A thin line of blood ran from his forehead, between his eyes to the end of his nose.

"Is he dead?" Pickle whispered.

"Drunk is what he is," Price said. "Listen to him snore. Help me get him out."

"We can take him to the hospital, Price. He might be hurt."

"He's not hurt, Pickle. He needs more than a hospital."

"We ought to do something for him," the boy protested.

Price lifted under Sawyer's arms. He eased him to the ground and dragged him to the other side of the birch tree. He propped the Indian against it, his chin sagging down on his bare, brown chest. Price took his jacket off and slipped it around Sawyer's shoulders. He looked down with deepening grief. "Let's go, Pickle. There's nothing we can ever do for Sawyer Two Feathers."

|| 20 ||

"It ain't right," Pickle muttered.

"What ain't right?" Price asked.

"Nothing. I was just thinking."

"Well, while you're busy thinking, why don't you open that map beside you and tell me how to get to Hollywood. We're on Route Eighty-nine. I recollect it goes all the way through Utah. Then we shift over to another road to Las Vegas, and from there we head for Los Angeles. When you have figured all that out, you ought to go through the fifth-grade reader. You didn't do any studying at the cabin, and I heard you talking like a cracker half the time. You don't want to grow up like Sawyer and me."

"How's that, Price?"

"Left behind, Pickle, or left out, one or the other."

Pickle settled down to study his map. Now that he could read the names it made more sense to him. He wondered what some of those places were like as he spelled out the names. He had made up his mind that once he got his rig he would head back this way to check up on Two Feathers. Now he traced Route 89 with his finger to where it stopped heading for California and headed for, let's see, Arizona. He traced 89 back up to where they were. "What's this Great Salt Lake, Price?"

"I've heard you can't sink in it, I reckon. Have you found any parks we can stay overnight in, ones that don't have bears?"

"Lots of them," Pickle replied, "but the map don't tell me about bears."

"'Doesn't' tell you, Pickle. Get started on your reading while there's still some light."

Price drove steadily day after day. Pickle no longer fretted about driving. From time to time he spelled Price at the wheel, but he spent most of the days bent over the fifth-grade reader, sounding out the hard words, reading aloud when Price asked him to, and puzzling over the parts he didn't understand. Price was astonished at Pickle's determination. Pickle was smart enough in lots of ways, Price already knew; now he was becoming school smart. He wasn't going to have any trouble when he went back home if his pa would leave him be.

To Price, Las Vegas was only a place on the map. He was surprised that Pickle had heard of the place. His father had gone to some kind of a special meeting there a couple of years ago, he told Price. "He came home with a wad of bills in his pocket, bragging to Ma that he had showed the people at the table a thing or two about shooting craps. He wouldn't tell Ma how much he won. She kept after him to buy a new car, the De Soto was wearing out, but Pa never did."

It seemed to Price that Las Vegas was mostly a town with lots of lights, a couple of big hotels, and slot machines. They ate supper at the counter of a drugstore.

Pickle kept turning around on his stool, unable to keep his eyes off the slots against the wall.

"How much money we got left?" he asked Price at last.

"The same as we're going to have when we leave town."

"Aw, come on, Price. You saw what I did back in Jackson."

"I did. And I also heard what Two Feathers said, that none of those slot machines had paid off for a year before you came along. What if you'd gone in the Silver Dollar a week before you did, what about that?"

"That just proves I was lucky, Price. Like Pa."

"Did your pa tell you how much he lost in Las Vegas? I bet not. You lose more than you win gambling, but nobody likes to talk about that."

"Well, I ain't going to lose, you'll see."

The tired-looking woman behind the soda counter listened. "I play those machines all the time, Sonny. I'm hooked on them. When the manager pays me on Saturday, I get my money in rolls of quarters. They're gone by Sunday. Give the boy five dollars to play with, Mister," she said to Price. "When it's gone, drag him out of here and take him over to California. They don't have machines there."

Price handed the woman a five-dollar bill. Proudly Pickle took his quarters to the row of slot machines. He tested the handles of a couple. "Which one's ready, ma'am?" he called to the counter.

"All of them—and none of them," she replied.

Pickle put the first quarter in. And the second. And the third. On his next to last quarter, the machine coughed and spit out six quarters. Pickle shouted with excitement. He fed them back into the machine. That was that. Pickle whacked it with his fist. He slouched back to the counter.

"You finished your hamburger yet, Price? Let's get on the road. I'll drive for a while."

The old man at the service station where Las Vegas disappeared into the desert gave the Dodge a hard look. He asked if they were planning to go to Los Angeles. When Pickle nodded, he said, "You better keep on going tonight. This old truck might not make it in daytime. The temperature out there is apt to go up to a hundred and twenty in the middle of the day. It's just as hot as Death Valley this time of year."

He noticed Pickle's puzzlement. He looked at the Wisconsin plates. "I guess you never heard of Death Valley? It's up north a hundred miles or so, not too far. It's the hottest place in the whole country. That's official, too. Some scientist fellows went out there and proved it. Broke the thermometer, they say. It went right up to one hundred and twenty-five degrees and broke. They say they never did find out how hot it really was. They couldn't measure, could they, with a busted thermometer?"

The old man laughed. "You'll be all right, though. It cools down at night. You have a full tank of gas to see you through. That will be three dollars even. And don't get off the road. The sand along the shoulders will grab your tires, and they'll have to pull you out."

Pickle pushed the needle to forty-five and held it there. The headlights turned the asphalt strip a kind of ugly yellow ahead of the pickup. A long-eared rabbit bounded from the darkness and paused for a second in the middle of the road. Before Pickle could hit the brakes, it disappeared into the darkness on the other side.

Price pulled his straw hat down over his eyes and slouched in the corner. "You tell me when you get tired, Pickle, and I'll take over. It's two hundred and seventy miles, the man back there said."

Pickle didn't reply. He grasped the steering wheel and peered ahead. Two hundred and seventy miles, he thought. That's pretty far. He checked the speedometer. Forty-five miles every hour if he didn't stop. He began to puzzle over how long it would take to reach Los Angeles. Price probably knew, but he was bound if he was going to ask him. There had to be some way to find out. He added forty-five and forty-five. That made ninety. And two nineties, that was—he thought hard—that was one hundred eighty, four hours. Plus two more hours, ninety miles. That made it two hundred seventy. "Golddurn," he said under his breath, "that's just what the man said." He counted back, to be sure. Six hours, it *was* six hours. "Hey, Price," he exclaimed. "I figured it out. It's six hours to Hollywood. I did it in my head. Yes, sir. Forty-five times six is two hundred seventy. Did you know that?"

Price tipped his hat up. He reached out and squeezed Pickle's right arm. "I didn't know until now, Pickle. There's nothing you can't do when you think about it for a while. Now, you're going to wake me up when we're exactly halfway there. When will that be?"

The boy paused, then said, "Three hours."

"And how far down the road will we be when we're halfway there?"

"I knew you was going to ask that, Price. I already got it figured out. It's 135 miles, that's what it is."

"You got it, Pickle. Don't forget to wake me up."

Pickle didn't forget, but he didn't do it. Motionless behind the wheel, he followed the long straight road through the desert. Powerful automobiles raced past, their lights throwing shadows ahead of the Dodge. A big lizard scuttled under his wheels before Pickle could swerve. He felt a small bump under a front wheel. There was no point in stopping to see about the lizard, he thought sadly.

When he figured they had only forty-five or fifty miles to go, Pickle pulled over to the side, careful to keep the wheels on the asphalt. "Price," he said, "I reckon we're about there. You ready to take your turn?"

Price sat up and rubbed his eyes. It was cool now inside the cab. He reached under the seat for the canteen Pickle had bought in Crowheart. As he drank the tepid water, he started to count back the days to their picnic by the Wind River. He lost track. Shoot, he said to himself, echoing Pickle's favorite expression, what difference did it make? They had made it to California—or almost made it—which was what they had set out to do. Who would have thought, he mused, back in Lutherville at the garage, watching Clarence and Pickle go to work on the Bedford County truck, that he would end up in Hollywood, California? The more you thought about, the less sense it made, but he felt good about it, really good. He and Pickle and the Dodge, they had done it. A cracker farm boy and a black convict and a rusty old truck, they had made it.

Price kicked the door open. It had started to stick the last couple of days. Pickle said the tires were wearing thin, too. He stood in the sand and stretched. He walked around to the other side. "You done good, Pickle," he teased. "I'll wake you up as soon as I see a movie star."

Two hours later, just before dawn, Price parked the Dodge under a palm tree on a street filled with little white houses. Startled when the sound of the motor stopped, Pickle sat up, abruptly. "What's wrong, Price? How come you stopped?"

"We're here, Pickle. And I'm lost. I mean I know where I'm at, but I don't know where to go. Tell me what you had in mind, and I'll see if I can find it for you. What did your ma tell you about Hollywood?"

Pickle had already told Price almost everything he remembered Ma saying about Hollywood and the motion-picture stars. What else did she say? Pickle thought back to the bits and pieces of talk he heard from Ma and Myrna around her kitchen table.

"There's this movie house," he explained to Price, "where the movie stars put their feet in wet concrete and write their names. And there's a drugstore I told you nearby where if you want to be a star, you sit at the counter and wait to be discovered, Ma said."

"You figure on being a star, Pickle?"

"Nah, I just want to sit there and see one, so I can tell Ma about it."

"Well, let's find us an all-night diner. Maybe they'll know what you are talking about."

The woman in the diner laughed when Pickle tried to explain. "Just arrived in town, did you? Sure, I know where you want to go. If you get lost along the way, someone else will help you." She gave Price some complicated directions. When he shook his head in confusion, she wrote them down slowly on a scrap of paper.

Price looked at the paper outside. "I don't believe she got to the fifth grade either, Pickle." He showed the directions to Pickle.

"I can't read it. What does it say?"

"They don't make any sense to me, but I'll try to follow them," Price promised. "Let's get started before traffic picks up."

Two hours later, after losing their way countless times, Price pointed across a wide street. "There's the Chinese theater the woman told us about. You want to get out? The drugstore is down the street."

After Pickle tried to fit his boots in the concrete footprints, they went to the drugstore. They sat at the counter drinking another cup of coffee, feeling out of place. Neither Pickle nor Price dared say anything to the girl who served them.

"We must look like a couple of hicks," Price whispered. "How long do you figure on waiting for a star to come in? And how are you going to know it's a star?"

"I dunno." Pickle finished his coffee. He might as well ask one question. "Where do the movie stars live?" he inquired of the waitress.

"All over," the girl said. "You better take a tour bus. They start running at nine. You can find one a couple of blocks down the street. That's the best way," she assured Pickle.

As they pulled out in the street, Pickle noticed a funny-looking car ahead of him. It wasn't anything he recognized. There weren't any numbers on the license plate, just some letters. *G-A-B-L-E*, Gable. Gable, Clark Gable. He was all Ma talked about, Clark Gable and a picture called *Gone with the Wind*. She'd seen it four or five times already, twice with Myrna.

"Price, that car ahead. That's a movie star's car. Let's follow it and see where it goes. We won't have to take the tour bus."

Price slipped the truck up behind the car with the top down. When it turned right, Price turned right. When it sped up, Price put the accelerator to the floor. When it wound its way up a narrow curving road into the hills, Price stuck close behind. He saw the driver turn around to look back, sort of an old guy with a thin moustache and big floppy ears. The man smiled at the Dodge and gave a little wave. Then his car jumped ahead like a scared rabbit and disappeared around a turn. By the time Price made the turn, the car was gone.

Price slowed in front of a driveway. "What now, Pickle?" he asked.

Before Pickle could answer, a bolt of red flashed down the driveway and streaked into the side of the Dodge.

‖ 21 ‖

Pickle's eyelids fluttered. He blinked and closed his eyes. Things were blurry. He opened them again, slowly this time. He was on his back and his head seemed to be in someone's lap. Ma's? That didn't seem likely. Ma never held his head in her lap. And there was Price kneeling over him looking worried. Strangers were staring down at him from above. They came in and out of focus as he tried to recognize them. He was pretty sure he had never seen them before: a kind of fat woman in a flowery dress, a tall, thin man in white with yellow hair, and a black man in a dark gray suit standing back a little.

Pickle wrinkled his nose. He smelled perfume. Now he knew it wasn't Ma's lap. Ma's perfume was so strong Pa used to ask if she took a bath in it. This was a soft far-away smell. A cool hand brushed his hair off his forehead. A soft voice said, "He's waking up, Mama." A face leaned over his. Red lips moved. "Are you all right?" the mouth said.

Pickle could focus now. The sun was in back of the woman's face. He squinted to see who was holding his head. It was a young woman, and Pickle knew at once he had never seen anyone so beautiful in his life. He struggled to sit up. His head spun a mile a minute and he let it rest again in the woman's lap and closed his eyes. He heard her voice, sharper now and upset. "Why didn't you call the ambulance, Mama? He's hurt, you can see that. Call up Doctor Davis and tell him to get here with an ambulance."

Other voices from above. A voice, impatient, that didn't seem to care, the tall blond man's, maybe. "He's coming around, Becky. I doubt that we need to bother with the medical establishment."

Another voice, the flowery woman's, Pickle decided, hard and harsh. "Do you want me to call the police, too, Becky? Do you want me to tell them this is your third accident and one of the people you hit the last time is still in the hospital, telling her lawyer to sue you for everything you own? Let me remind you they took away your license. Do you want all that trouble, Becky? The boy's going to be all right. He had no business being in front of your driveway. He shouldn't have been out on the road stargazing in a broken-down old truck that was a menace to society."

Finally, a voice he recognized. "I'd thank you to call a doctor, ma'am. I'd like to have a doctor see him. He might be hurt real bad, and we wouldn't know about it."

Pickle sat up again. He wasn't so dizzy this time. "Nah, Price," he managed to say, "I don't need no doctor." He felt his head where it throbbed. "It ain't no worse than when I got hit with a baseball once. Shoot, I'm ready to go."

He tried to stand. His legs were weak. Price held him steady while Pickle took a few steps.

"See, Price? I don't need me no doctor." He took Price's arm. "And we don't need any police either. We'll go on about our business. We don't want to trouble these folks no more." Shoot, he thought, the last thing he and Price needed was the police asking them questions.

"We're not going anywhere in the Dodge, Pickle." Price turned Pickle around to face the road. The truck was sitting in the driveway, oil and water dripping from underneath. It sagged like a broken board. Pickle's door was hammered in. In back of the Dodge was a little red roadster, its front smashed to pieces.

"Gosh," Pickle said. "Are you all right?" he asked the woman who had held his head in her lap. He saw that she was dressed in white like the tall man. Her brown hair was tied back with a kerchief.

"Oh, I'm all right. It's always other people who get hurt. I have a lucky star watching over me. Sometimes, anyway."

"We pushed them out of the way," Price explained. "Mr? . . ." He looked toward the man in the gray suit, which was sort of like a uniform.

"Jethro," the man said. "I'm the chauffeur."

"Mr. Jethro and Mr. . . ." Price paused again.

"Hope." The blond man told Price. "Conrad Hope. I'm Becky's husband."

"And Mr. Hope pushed the Dodge and Mrs. Hope's car off the road."

"My name isn't Mrs. Hope," the young woman objected. "Conrad is my husband. My name is Becky Church. I've always been Becky Church."

"Yes, we know, Becky," her husband said in a tired voice. "We all understand that you are Becky Church. Now, could we finish our tennis game you ran out on? Later, we can discuss this situation. Jethro and . . ." He looked at Price.

"Douglas, Price Douglas."

"Douglas will look after things. What's the boy's name?"

"John Sherburn," Price replied. "Can you walk now?" he asked Pickle. "I'll help you up the driveway."

Becky Church. The name sounded familiar to Pickle. He could hear Ma talking to Myrna at the table, words like, "And Becky Church was Clark Gable's daughter in that picture. She wasn't no more than ten years old, but she made Clark look like a wooden Indian. You were too young to see it, Myrna, but we'll go soon as it comes back. I left you with Aunt Vinnie and went to the picture show by myself."

"You're Becky Church?" he asked the young woman.

The fat woman spoke before Becky Church could reply. "She is. She's my only daughter."

"The movie star?" Pickle persisted.

"All her life she was a star," her mother replied. "Ever since she made *Tom Sawyer,* her first picture, when she was eight years old. And I was right there with you, wasn't I, dear?"

Becky Church didn't answer. She started to walk, arms folded tightly, up the driveway toward a great white palace. Price and Pickle followed. Conrad Hope and Mrs. Church, whispering to each other, trailed behind.

"Miss Becky doesn't make pictures anymore," Jethro explained to Price and Pickle. "She quit three years ago. Her mother didn't like that one bit, I can tell you. 'What about your public?' she kept asking. 'You owe them something.' What she meant was 'What about me?'"

They were sitting in folding chairs in the shadow of a

huge six-door garage, one door of which was rolled up. Beyond the garage lay the gardens and, Jethro said, a pool and a tennis court. Price could hear a ball bouncing back and forth.

A Japanese man in a white jacket had brought three trays with lunch on them. Pickle was feeling as good as ever now, except for a lump over his right ear. He listened carefully to the chauffeur tell them about Becky Church. He would really have something to tell Ma and Myrna.

Price listened, too, mostly because he had to, not because he was much interested in the real life story of a child movie star. He had never been to a picture show in his life until he was in the work camp. Once a month, on a Sunday evening, Barnett put a sheet on the wall of the eating room, and showed some streaky, flickering pictures. It was always the same picture about a cowboy and his horse, Trigger, and his girlfriend.

What Price was more concerned about was the pickup. Jethro had called a tow truck to take away the two wrecks. He was pretty certain they couldn't do anything with the Dodge. Jethro had taken their things out, including the brown envelope with their money. The piece of canvas, the mattress, and the bags were piled neatly in the garage; Price had slipped the envelope into his suitcase. The last time he counted, they still had over a thousand dollars inside. They'd have to use some of it now to take the bus home.

"I used to live upstairs," Jethro said. "There's an apartment for the chauffeur over the garage. I drove Miss Becky and her mother to the studio and brought them home. And I looked after all the cars Mrs. Church had made Becky buy."

There were five cars lined up in the garage, Pickle knew. He had already sneaked a look.

"Then Miss Becky quit the pictures and started getting married and driving herself, even after she lost her license. She told me she didn't need me all the time. She likes little sports cars. I bought a home down in the city and got married myself. Every night I drive a different car home to keep it tuned up."

"Gosh," Pickle said. "Is that all the driving they get?"

"Just about. If Mrs. Church wants to go somewhere, I take her, generally in the Chrysler. Mr. Hope uses her Rolls-Royce."

"What about her pa, do you drive him?" Pickle wanted to know.

"He died three years ago, but he didn't live here long. He and Mrs. Church were divorced. He kept track of Miss Becky's money for her. He invested it and put it in a trust where Mrs. Church couldn't get at it. By now she must be as rich—Miss Becky, I mean—as John D. Rockefeller."

Jethro liked talking about Becky Church. Price figured he was bored sitting around the garage all day waiting to take Mrs. Church shopping. "It's a mighty big house," he said. "How big is it, Mr. Jethro?"

"I've only been in the kitchen. There's a Japanese couple and a Mexican woman who look after it. We don't talk much. Once, they say, it was the biggest house in Hollywood. It belonged to a silent-movies star who went broke and killed himself. Mr. Church bought the place cheap. It's not Miss Becky's yet."

"What do you mean?" Price asked. He was realizing he liked to talk about money ever since they collected some from old Bertha Loftus and he took charge of it for

Pickle and himself. He wondered if they had courses at the university where they taught you about money, how to get it, and how to make it grow.

"Everything is in the trust. Miss Becky and her mother—and Mr. Hope, too, I think—get a big allowance until she is twenty-five. Then everything is Miss Becky's. That's two years from now. Her mother and Mr. Hope are worried sick. Either way they lose. If something happens to Miss Becky, like an accident, everything goes to a charity, except for a little bit to her mother. And after she turns twenty-five Miss Becky can do what she wants. She doesn't like her mother or her husband much these days. She doesn't know what she's going to do when she's twenty-five, she told me one day."

"How come she fights with her mother?" Pickle never dared fight with Ma, and Myrna didn't have to.

"Miss Becky says her mother brought her up like a slave, and she had no life of her own. Her mother says she made her daughter into a star. Back and forth they go at it. Now that Mr. Hope is here, he takes Mrs. Church's side. That makes Miss Becky even madder."

Price had a low opinion of the tall, thin man who called him Douglas in a funny accent.

"Miss Becky doesn't listen to him any more than she listens to her mother. She says he married her for her money. He probably did. He used to play a piano in a night club. He says he's from an aristocratic English family, but I know for a fact he grew up around here. I reckon he's going to wait until Miss Becky is twenty-five to see what happens. The other two husbands didn't wait."

"Why doesn't she make movies anymore?" Pickle asked.

"She quit when her father died. I think it was to spite her mother. She blamed her mother for the divorce. I don't know about that. He was probably more interested in her money than he was in his daughter. You can't blame him, though. He made Miss Becky about as rich as anyone in Hollywood. The fact is I can't see why she wants to kill herself before she's twenty-five."

A Japanese woman came out of the house. Without a word she gathered the trays and took them inside. Pickle left Price and Jethro and went into the garage. He had caught a glimpse of a touring car that looked like a car he had seen once before.

It *was* like the one at the Pure Oil station, a sixteen-cylinder Cadillac, one of the last ones they made, Pickle bet. He wasn't exactly certain what year that was, but he knew they didn't make them anymore. He and Pa tried to keep track of which cars they stopped making and which new ones they started making, like the Kaiser and the Frazier. There weren't too many big cars in Lutherville to keep track of. The ones they did see were cars from up north headed for Florida that stopped for a tank of gas.

At Jenkins's Pure Oil station, they had seen their first and only sixteen-cylinder Cadillac. "Look at that one, Pickle," Pa said when they passed the station. He turned the Dodge around in the middle of the road and went back to have a good look. "It's a sixteen-cylinder Cadillac," he said. "I heard they don't make them anymore."

They had walked around the big car, admiring its whitewall tires and the twin spares tucked into the front fenders. There were all kinds of gauges and buttons on the wooden dash, and a clock that was working. When

Pickle peered inside, he sniffed the smell of lavender, like Aunt Vinnie kept in her bureau drawers.

"How fast will she go, Mister?" Pickle had asked the man who came out of the station drinking a Coca-Cola.

"Faster than I've ever taken her," the man had replied. "She'll do over a hundred, I'm certain of that. This year I'm thinking of stopping over at Daytona to see what she'll do on the beach."

"Did you hear that, Pickle, a hundred?" Pa had said. "That's really something, ain't it?"

Pickle could hardly wait to get back home to tell Pa about the Cadillac. Pa wasn't so bad when they talked about cars and shooting craps and cockfights. It was the strappings that drove them apart. Maybe he did deserve a walloping once in a while for not paying attention in school, but Pa had no call to beat him as hard as he did. When he saw how much Pickle had learned over the summer, he might let up a little. He better not tell Pa he took the Dodge. Let him think someone else took it. He'd just say he hitched across the country with another boy he met on the road.

Now, in the dim interior of Becky Church's six-car garage, Pickle eased himself behind the wheel of a sixteen-cylinder Cadillac, a shining, dark green car with a tan canvas top and silver tire covers over the spares. He discovered a radio. Pickle turned the knob. Not a sound. He turned another knob. Shoot, not a sound.

"You have to turn the motor on, John," Jethro told him. He reached in to turn the ignition key. "Start it up," he said.

The motor caught at once and settled down to a quiet, rich purr. The Cadillac didn't shake like the old Dodge. The radio squawked. Hastily, Pickle turned it off. He leaned back against the leather seat. He closed his hands around the burnished steering wheel. "Whirrr," he said softly.

"It's a fine automobile," Jethro said. "Like new, almost, only ten thousand miles. I like it the best of all, but Mrs. Church says it makes her hair blow, even with the top up. She takes the Rolls or the Chrysler. Miss Becky likes fast little cars." Jethro turned the lights on in the garage. He took a cloth and started to dust the cars. Pickle watched. Becky Church sure was rich.

Pickle heard the sound of arguing outside. He slipped out of the Cadillac. In the driveway Becky Church was sort of walking backward toward the garage, shouting at her mother and Conrad Hope, who were following her. They were talking back loudly, telling Becky that she couldn't do something.

"Mama," Becky was saying. "Let me do something for myself once. I talked to Mr. Roscoe, and he said I could if I wanted to. They are *mine*, Mama. I can do what I want with them."

"But, Becky," Mr. Hope said, "I agree with your mother. We cannot permit this foolish gesture."

"You are not in a position to permit or not permit anything," Becky Church told her husband nastily. "You have your allowance, like the rest of us, and a place to live. You and Mama can't tell me how to live my life. Anytime you want to leave, I'll be deliriously happy to give you any car in the garage to leave in, including that Rolls-Royce. The same goes for you, too, Mama."

"Becky, be reasonable. We are only interested in your welfare," her mother said.

"Papa was the only one interested in my welfare, Mama, and he's gone. Please leave me be. Sometimes, I don't think I'll ever live to be twenty-five, if you don't leave me be." Becky's voice rose again. "I'm going to do it. I ruined their truck, and I'm going to replace it."

"Not the Rolls, Becky, please," Conrad Hope begged. "I rather fancy the Rolls."

"Or the Chrysler, please, honey. It's the only one I feel comfortable in," her mother pleaded.

"All right, not the Rolls and not the Chrysler. Now let me talk to them without bothering me. Please!"

Becky turned to see Pickle standing at the back of the Cadillac, pretending he hadn't heard. "Oh, there you are. Your name is Sherburn, right? Where's your friend?"

"Yes, ma'am, John Sherburn. Price is Price Douglas. He was here a minute ago."

"See if you can find him, please. I want to talk to you both. He may be at the swimming pool. It's over there." Becky pointed beyond the house. "You can use it any time you want."

Pickle found Price beside an enormous blue-tiled pool. It seemed to Pickle to be bigger than the pond in back of Aunt Vinnie's house where he swam sometimes in the summer. It dried up in August unless it rained a lot. "Hey, Price," he called. "Miss Becky said we could swim there if we want. Right now she needs to talk to us."

"I feel responsible for your truck," Becky said. "I can give you some money, enough for two tickets to Wisconsin plus whatever you say the truck was worth. Is that where you want to go?"

"Well," Price stammered. How to explain that neither one of them lived in Wisconsin?

"Or," Becky said, "you can have one of the cars in the garage. I hate them. Mama bought one whenever she was bored, so I could go to the studio in style, she said. I'm not going to the studio anymore. These cars are just sitting here like circus elephants for Jethro to go back and forth in. Do you want one? Mr. Roscoe—he's in charge of my affairs—says it's all right. He'll take care of the details." Becky looked at Pickle. "You heard what Mama and Conrad said, didn't you? You can't have the Rolls or the Chrysler."

"I heard," Pickle said, embarrassed. "I didn't know what a Rolls was."

"A Rolls-Royce. It's the most expensive car in the world. We bought it as a wedding present for Conrad to use. That was a mistake. I don't know what the other cars are."

Pickle knew. "There's a Buick, that's the roadster, and a Chrysler Imperial, and a Lincoln Continental, and this here Cadillac." He rested his hand lovingly on the back of the touring car.

"This is the one you like, isn't it, John? What about you, Douglas?"

Price felt an urge to tell Becky Church, movie star or no movie star, he wasn't her chauffeur, but he didn't. The look in Pickle's eyes as he gazed at the big, green touring car was enough to let Miss Church call him Douglas to the end of the time if she wanted to. Shoot, he thought, we'll leave this crazy place and drive back in style.

"John is the car expert," he said. "I'll go along with what he says. And we do thank you, ma'am. You don't have to do it, you know, Miss Church. We have more than enough money to get home on the bus. It was half my fault, anyway, for slowing down in front of your driveway."

"We were chasing Clark Gable," Pickle said, "but we couldn't keep up."

"So it was Clark's fault, was it?" Becky laughed. "That lets us both off the hook. We'll go tell him about it tomorrow if he isn't doing a picture. I haven't seen him in the longest time.

"Now I have to call Mr. Roscoe to transfer the car over to one of you. You?" she asked Price, "or you, John? Whose is it to be? You're a little young, aren't you, John? But I guess it's all right to own a car, even if you can't drive it. I'll ask Mr. Roscoe about that."

"Maybe to both of us, then," Pickle said.

"Give me your address in Wisconsin, please," Becky took a piece of paper and silver pen from the pocket of her blouse.

Darn, Price said to himself. They had to get things straight now as best they could. "John's from down South, ma'am, and I live in Detroit now. I used to live near John's place." That was the truth at least. "We were both hitching across the country and a man in Madison, Wisconsin, gave us that old pickup for helping us clean out his place."

"He already had a new Ford and old Packard," Pickle said. "He didn't need the Dodge no more."

Becky Church wasn't interested in the details. "Here," she said, handing Price the paper and pen, "name, address, birth date and driver's license—if you have one. Give the paper to Jethro and he'll take it to Mr. Roscoe."

Pickle wasn't certain where he lived. He didn't want to write down the county work farm. He thought for a minute. Carefully he wrote, "John Pickel Sherburn, County Farm Road, Lutherville." That ought to do it.

Becky glanced at the paper. "That looks okay. Mr. Roscoe says it will take a couple of days, and you'll have to sign something later. Jethro will bring whatever it is to you. Where are you staying?"

Jethro answered the question. "They haven't found a place yet, Miss Becky. Could they have my place over the garage?"

"Fine," she replied, "you can stay over the garage, unless"—she looked at Pickle—"you want me to find you a room in the big house."

"No, ma'am," Pickle replied. "I'll stay with Price out here."

‖22‖

"She didn't mean any harm," Jethro explained to Price. "It's hard for her to think of anyone except herself."

"Nobody ever means any harm," Price said bitterly, "but they hurt all the same. She gives me half of a ten-thousand dollar car, or whatever that car cost, and a kick at the same time. Two Feathers was right."

"Two Feathers?" Jethro asked.

"An Indian we met along the way. He said folks like us couldn't ever get out from under."

"Miss Becky and her mama are both good to me," said Jethro. "Mr. Hope lets me know who I am, but he won't be here much longer. Do you want to see the apartment? Right up the steps there. I'll bring your bags along."

"We can carry our own," Pickle told him. "They don't weigh nothing."

"The sofa turns into a bed," Jethro said as he showed them a sitting room between the bedroom and a tiny kitchen and bath. "I come here and sit sometimes when there's nothing for me to do."

He opened the bureau drawers. "Here's some clothes Miss Becky's second husband left behind. She said I could have them, but they don't fit me." He held up some swimming trunks. "There's a couple of bathing suits if you use the pool. I guess it's all right if Miss Becky said so."

"Where did her second husband go?" Pickle asked. The big house didn't look like the kind of place you'd walk away from.

"Down to Mr. Roscoe's office to get his money, I suppose," Jethro said. "That was Mr. Wheeler. He cost Miss Becky a pretty penny, according to her mother. Take the clothes if you want them. Mr. Wheeler was about Mr. Douglas's size."

"My name is Price."

"I heard. I'm Jethro Spokes." He held his hand out to Price, then Pickle. "I'll be in the garage if you want me."

"This is a pretty good place," Pickle said, "the best we've done so far. Why don't we go swimming in Miss Becky's pool, Price? Nobody ever uses it, Jethro said. Wouldn't that be something, to have your own swimming pool?" He took the swimming trunks from the drawer. "Which one do you want?"

"It doesn't matter. The blue-and-white one, I guess. We can change in a little house by the pool."

"I'll change here," Pickle said. "Then I can jump right in." He broke ahead of Price as they crossed the lawn toward the pool. He raced to the edge and without missing a step hurled himself far out into the water. His head broke the surface. "Did you see that, Price? Come on in. It's real warm. I'm going off the diving board." He swam to the other end with awkward, powerful strokes.

Price sat at the edge of the shallow end, letting his legs hang into the water. He wasn't much of a swimmer. He could keep his head above water, that was about it.

"I'll sit here in the sun for a while and watch," he called to Pickle.

Pickle jumped from the diving board again and again, shouting each time for Price to watch him. Mr. Hope appeared from the direction of the house. He came down to where Price was sitting.

"Did Jethro say you could use the pool?" he demanded.

Price shook his head.

"You are using it without asking?"

Price shook his head again. He didn't feel obliged to answer.

"Then who said you could be here?"

"Miss Church told John, I believe."

"You're sure of that?"

Price nodded.

"I see," Conrad Hope said. He walked back toward the house.

Pickle swam to where Price was and pulled himself out of the water. "What did he want?"

"He wanted to know who said we could use the pool. I told him Miss Church said so. Is that right?"

"Yep. I'm going to get me one of those towels in the little house. You want one?"

"I'm not going to get wet. Thanks anyway."

Pickle dived deep into the pool. He came up for air just shy of the diving board. He went into the cabana and came out drying his head with a towel. He almost bumped into Becky Church.

She said something to Pickle that Price couldn't hear. She sat down at a little white table with a striped umbrella over it. She pushed a chair out with her foot for Pickle to sit in. Becky said something else and smiled. Pickle shrugged. He didn't answer. Becky pointed to the cabana. Pickle shook his head.

What was going on? Price wondered. Whatever it was, Pickle didn't look comfortable. Becky Church said something else, leaning across the table toward Pickle. Pickle shook his head. It looked to Price as though he was blushing. He pushed the chair back. Price heard the metal scrape the tile. Pickle plunged into the pool. Becky Church stood up. She stared after Pickle for a moment, then disappeared behind a hedge.

"What was that all about?" Price asked.

"Nothing."

"It must have been something. Miss Church was talking a lot."

"Yeah."

"But you weren't saying much."

"Nah."

Price didn't press. Pickle would tell him in his good time if he wanted to. All Price was interested in now was leaving. He felt out of place on Miss Church's estate or whatever it was. While they waited for the Cadillac's papers, he decided Pickle would get some real teaching. The boy's writing wasn't good, and his spelling was worse. They would work on those.

Having their breakfast on trays the Japanese man had brought up to the apartment, Price read what Pickle had written the night before. It was about their visit to the Silver Dollar bar in Jackson. "This is a good story, Pickle, but a lot of the words are spelled wrong. You are supposed to spell 'machine' with a *ch,* not an *sh.*"

"You said to spell 'shoot' with an *sh,*" Pickle reminded him.

"That's different," Price said without thinking.

"What's different about it? It sounds the same."

Price was trapped. Teaching was a hard business. He had about used up everything he learned in high school.

"I can't tell you, Pickle. It's just different. You have to learn to spell these words the way they come."

Pickle drank the last drop of coffee. "Do you suppose I could go over to the kitchen and ask for another cup of coffee? You want one, too?"

"Why not?" Price said. "Shall I come with you?"

"I reckon I can ask for two cups of coffee by myself."

"I'm sorry, Pickle. Sure you can. I don't feel good about this place. It makes me fret."

"Me, too," Pickle said. "I can't wait to get my hands on the wheel of that Cadillac. Once we take off, we won't have to stop until we get there. There's lots of room to sleep in the backseat."

"I'll have to stop somewhere and catch the bus to Detroit. We can find a place on the map later."

"I'll drive you back home," Pickle said. "I drove you there, didn't I?"

"Not this time, Pickle. I'm responsible for you, whether you like it or not, and I'm seeing that you get to Lutherville, or pretty close, anyway."

Pickle carried the two trays down the steps. He banged on the back door of the house. He heard soft voices inside he couldn't understand. The Japanese man came to the door. He pointed to a button beside the door. He pushed it. A chime rang inside. He took the tray from Pickle.

"Can we have some coffee, please?" Pickle asked.

The man stared at Pickle. "Coffee?" he repeated.

Pickle nodded. "Two cups, milk and sugar, too."

"Milk and sugar?"

What was wrong with the guy? Pickle thought. How

come he had to repeat everything? "Milk and sugar, yeah," he said.

"Very good," the Japanese said. "You wait here. Coffee, milk, and sugar."

As Pickle took the trays, Becky Church came out the door. "I thought I heard your voice, John. Is everything all right in the apartment?"

"Yes, ma'am, we're fine."

"I'm getting a new car this morning, John. Another MG, light blue. It's the only color they had. I prefer red, really."

Pickle was interested. He had never heard of an MG. "What kind of car is that?" he asked.

"Oh, it's an English sports car, a two seater, like the red one I drove into you."

"That's nice. I'd like to see it."

"I was thinking we could drive up to Clark Gable's place. I'll blow the horn when I'm ready."

"Okay," Pickle said. "I'll tell Price. I have to take the coffee back now. I'm doing my lessons."

"The MG has only two seats. I'm not sure there's room for another person."

"I guess I better not, Miss Church. I promised to do my lessons all day. Some days on the road I didn't study as much as I should have."

Becky Church frowned. "As you like, John, as you like. I'll probably be too busy to get to Clark's anyway." She turned to go inside.

Price was sitting on Pickle's sofa bed talking into the telephone. He motioned to Pickle to put the coffee on the little table. Pickle heard him say, "It looks like I'll be all right then. I'll get a job in the afternoons to pay you for my board and keep." He listened some more, then answered, "I don't rightly know. It depends on when we get the car. As soon as I can anyway. Not more than two weeks. I'll see you soon."

Pickle figured Price was talking to his sister. They wouldn't let him and Myrna use the phone at home. Ma said it was for grown-ups. Not that Pickle had any use for it, anyway.

"That was Ruth," Price told him.

"You telephoned all the way to Detroit?" Pickle asked.

"I'll leave some money here to pay for it. Ruth and George had a phone put in just before I got home. Ruth gave me the number to keep. I won't have any trouble with Freckles, she said. The police arrested him holding up a store. He had a gun. He's going to be in jail for a while."

"That's good," Pickle said. He studied the black telephone sitting at the end of the sofa. "Do you reckon I can call up Aunt Vinnie?" he asked shyly.

"Do you have the number?"

Pickle shook his head.

"You never told me where she lived. It was always, 'Over at Aunt Vinnie's.'"

"Just the other side of Lutherville. She's got a phone all right. Ma called her up every day she didn't go over."

"What's her name, Pickle, so the operator can find her?"

"Jordan is her last name."

"Is she married? Maybe her husband has the phone."

"Marsh is her husband's name, Uncle Marsh. He's never home. He has his own rig. He goes everywhere. He's got to teach me how to handle it when I'm sixteen. He promised."

"I'll try," Price said. He dialed the operator and gave her the information. He heard strange nosises, remote voices, buzzes and hums, and, at last, a ringing. He handed the phone to Pickle.

"Aunt Vinnie? Is that you? This is Pickle." That was all he had a chance to say. Pickle leaned back on the sofa bed to listen.

Price went to the garage to talk to Jethro, who was preparing the Cadillac for its new owners. Jethro explained to Price what the buttons and gauges meant. "You'll have to watch the gas," he warned. "It has a big tank, but it uses a lot of gas. Everything else ought to be all right. I took it home last night. It ran like a gold watch. I'll be sorry to see it go. I came to work for Miss Becky when they bought this car. That was in 1939, the last year they made sixteen cylinders. All the stars had one, so her mother had to have one for Miss Becky, too. Afterward, Becky wouldn't trade it in for some reason. 'Mama's white elephant,' she called it. 'Course it's green, but it was always 'Mama's white elephant.' I'm sort of surprised she let it go."

Pickle thundered down the steps. "Price!" he shouted. "We got to leave now. Pa's not home. Ma and Myrna are staying at Aunt Vinnie's. Pa is back in the army."

"Calm down, Pickle. We'll leave tomorrow or the next day, no later. Your pa's not home?"

"The army called him back with the reserves. He's going to Korea or somewhere. Ma's all upset. She wants me home. I better go quick. Ma don't know how to do for herself. She needs a man in the house."

Price asked Jethro, "Can Mr. Roscoe speed up papers?"

|| 23 ||

The Cadillac *did* run like a gold watch. It was heavy, and Price felt as they left Los Angeles that it probably wasn't the fastest car on the road, but it was big and comfortable, no question about that. Jethro had put the top down, and the warm air flowed over them when Price pushed the speed to forty-five. Put the top back up in the desert, Jethro had said, or you'll have sunstroke.

Pickle squirmed in the front seat, complaining that he wanted a chance to see what the Cadillac could do.

"As soon as we get out of traffic, Pickle, we'll trade places. You're not back home yet. You heard Miss Church's mother say she lost her license."

"That's different," Pickle mumbled. "She didn't know how to drive those little cars. Jethro said only your name was on the papers."

"That's because we're in a hurry. You're a minor, Pickle—that means you're under legal age—and Mr. Roscoe needed more information to put you on the registration. Jethro showed me where to sign; I can turn the car over to you anytime. You can take care of the rest of it in Lutherville. Then it will be yours, all legal and proper."

"Are you sure it will take us four whole days?" The

day before, Pickle wasn't able to do his lessons. He squirmed in the chair and talked to himself and fussed at Price. "I can't study. Ma doesn't know how to do for her and Myrna. I have to get home."

Mr. Roscoe had hurried. Jethro was back the next day at midmorning with the title and registration and a letter of transfer and some other papers tucked in a leather case. Jethro backed the Cadillac out of the garage and pointed it down the drive. They could see for the first time how big it really was. It was like a battleship. Jethro handed the keys to Price. "Wait a minute," he told them. "Miss Becky said she wanted to say good-bye when you were ready to leave."

Miss Church reached over the door to shake Price's hand. "I'm very sorry about the truck, Douglas. I hope the white elephant gets you home."

She walked around to Pickle's side. In a thick southern accent, she said, "You take care, John, and be sure to come back and see me, hear?" Then she leaned into the car and gave Pickle a big kiss on the cheek.

Becky Church and Jethro stood in front of the garage waving as the Cadillac rolled down the drive, paused, and turned left onto the road.

Pickle spit on his hand and rubbed his cheek. "Shoot," he muttered. "I sure ain't going to tell Ma about that."

"Say it proper, Pickle."

"I'm not going to tell my mother about that."

"What are you going to tell her then? She'll want to know everything about Becky Church. Are you going to tell her you have a movie-star girlfriend who said you were kind of cute and that you could use her swimming pool and cabana as long as you wanted to? And asked you if maybe you wouldn't be more comfortable in the big house?"

Pickle's mouth dropped open. "How did you know?"

"Because it was the only thing to know. Becky Church is lonely. And she wants people to pay attention to her and love her, just like in the pictures. That's what Jethro said."

"Durn." If Price knew that, then it was time to tell him what he had figured out when they left Madison.

"How come you didn't tell me it was Professor Plum's mother you found in the trunk of the Packard? She wasn't going to hurt you."

Price's jaw sagged. "You knew, did you? I was scared. Not of ghosts, mind you—I don't believe in ghosts—but of the professor. There was no telling what he might have done if he thought we found out about his mother."

"She must have died a long time ago," Pickle said, "and he put her in the trunk there instead of in the ground. That ain't—isn't—so crazy. He probably loved her, don't you reckon, and didn't want her to go away?"

"That's what I reckon, too, Pickle. I'll keep your secret if you keep mine." He pulled the Cadillac to the side of the road. "Agreed, Pickle?"

Pickle threw open the door. "Agreed," he shouted. "Let me have the wheel of this baby. I'll have something to tell Pa when he gets home. I'll be able to tell him I drove a sixteen-cylinder Cadillac straight across Death Valley. Won't that be something?"

It was back to baloney sandwiches and RC Cola in the back of the touring car, under a tree or down a deserted road. There was no point in causing trouble now, Price told Pickle, when he protested that he wanted a hamburger with fries and a cup of coffee in a diner or roadside shack.

"They don't want me sitting at a counter next to their customers; you saw what happened in Jackson. When we show up in the biggest car in the county with California plates, we're going to catch trouble, no two ways about it. We're back in your part of the country, Pickle. They don't like us black people any better up in Detroit, but they don't take exception to us in their restaurants and buses and schools."

"I'd tell them that—" Pickle began.

"You'll tell them nothing because we aren't going to upset them. You're not dumb enough to stick your head in a hornet's nest, are you, Pickle?"

Price drove four hours, then gave the wheel to Pickle, who drove the next four. They dozed in the front seat or stretched out on the leather seat in back, heads on a soft wool traveling rug Jethro had left in the car, straw hats over their faces.

Late one afternoon, Price told Pickle they had crossed the Mississippi River. "Just like Huck Finn in a book I read. You're not too far from home now."

He stopped the car to look at his map, measuring the distance with his thumb and middle finger. "It's about four hundred miles, I calculate. How long will it take us, Pickle?"

They were driving at forty miles an hour to save gas. "Ten hours," Pickle announced at once. He glanced at the illuminated clock on the instrument panel. "That's about two o'clock—in the middle of the night."

"It will be later than that," Price said. "I have to get to a bus station. I think I've found the town. It's about sixty miles north of Lutherville, right on the main highway. Can you get home from there by yourself?"

"I reckon I can. I did it before, didn't I, headed north?"

"You had me to tell you what to do then," Price teased.

"Yeah, that's what you keep telling me," Pickle replied. He was quiet. It came to him for the first time that the trip to California was almost over. He was headed one way and Price Douglas another way. "Shoot, it ain't right, it just ain't right," he told himself.

"What ain't right, Pickle?"

"Nothing. I was just thinking about being by myself again."

"You'll find friends at school if you stop messing around. You'll have lots of friends. The teachers will jump you a couple of grades when they find out you can do your work like the other kids."

"Who's going to teach me, those old hens with spit curls who think Myrna is so smart?"

"You'll be all right, Pickle. Show them you can do the work. They'll pay attention to you then."

Afternoon became dusk which became night. Price reached into the paneled glove compartment for his cigarettes. The packet was empty. He had been smoking a lot more, he realized, since they left California. What was he going to do without the boy to look after? He would be the young guy now; Ruth would be after him all the time to do this or that, just like their mother. What would happen when the kids at high school heard he was an ex-convict, and they would find out soon enough? What was the point of going on to the university? It was pretty nice cruising around without having to do anything. He was free, absolutely free—almost. Was that what he really wanted? It probably was, but, he sighed, he would have to earn it. That was for goldarn sure, he'd have to earn it. Right now he needed a Lucky Strike.

"The next town we come to, pull in to see if a drugstore is open," he asked Pickle. "I'm out of cigarettes."

"Okay. I think I'll try one, too. The big kids at school smoke."

"You will not try one, too. As soon as I get home, Ruth is going to stop me. She made George stop years ago."

Pickle swung off the highway onto a narrow county road that became the main street of a small, sleeping town. The street was deserted. There was a light in the window of the drugstore. He pulled over across the street. "I'll go on down and turn around and pick you up," he told Price. They didn't take chances on turning the Cadillac around in the middle of main streets.

Pickle drove beyond town to a side road. He pulled in and backed around. He saw a policeman with a flashlight walking down the sidewalk toward the drugstore. Where had he come from? Pickle hadn't seen any police car. He brought the Cadillac to a halt and cut the lights.

He saw Price hammering on the door of the drugstore. The lights went out inside. Now he could hear Price hammer harder. The policeman went up to Price. He shone the light in his face. He said something. Price didn't pay any attention. He pushed past the officer into the middle of the street. The policeman drew his pistol. Price turned and marched ahead of the man down the road. In a minute the light disappeared.

Pickle waited. Slowly, lights out, he drove the Cadillac to where the two had disappeared. A dim light shone through the window of a white frame building. The police station, Pickle told himself. He kept on going and parked the Cadillac well off the road in front of a tractor.

They weren't going to turn Price loose, you could count on that. The officer probably figured Price was getting ready to bust into the store. Or maybe he got mad when Price pushed him aside. It didn't matter, they were going to keep him for a while. Tomorrow they'd book him for something and sooner or later discover he had a record. Pickle stopped thinking.

He reached around in back of the seat for his kit bag. He took Pa's pistol from under his extra clothes. He made sure the safety was on. He dropped it into his jacket pocket. He pulled the brim of his straw hat low over his eyes. He pulled the collar of his jacket up.

The deputy was sitting in a chair, his feet on the desk. He had half a bottle of Coca-Cola in his hand. He was almost asleep. The door to the cells in back was open. A single light bulb hung from the ceiling in both rooms. Pickle stood in the doorway. He reached in his pocket for the gun. He switched the safety off. He pointed it at the startled officer. "Back there!" Pickle ordered. He pointed the gun toward the cells.

The deputy opened his mouth, thought better of it, and rose to his feet. He went through the door.

"Let him out."

The policeman took a ring of keys from his belt. He unlocked the barred door and stood to one side. Price came out.

"In!" Pickle commanded. "Give me the keys." He pushed the door shut. He moved the pistol to his left hand. He found the key and locked the door. "Let's go," he said to Price. He had a sudden idea. "Hurry," he added. "I got the pickup running outside."

|| 24 ||

"Didn't nobody see the car, Price, I'm morally certain, but you better climb in back anyway."

Price dropped into the back. He stretched his long legs between the two little folded seats and leaned against the seat. He was trembling. "You're going to stay here a long time, boy," the policeman had said. "You struck an officer of the law and resisted arrest."

Helpless, Price had not replied. He crept into the cell like a whipped dog. He was trapped. Then that crazy Pickle came in waving a gun like the cowboy in the movie they showed every Sunday at the camp and rescued him. He was free again. He said a silent prayer of thanks. Now all he had to do was get home to Detroit. He'd be safe there. Ruth and George would see to that.

"Was that your pa's pistol you stole?"

Pickle was intent on seeing what lay ahead and what lay behind. Every five seconds he peered into the rearview mirror. "Yeah," he answered.

Price pushed down one of the jump seats and leaned forward, his arms folded on the top of the front seat. He looked anxiously down the road. The clock reached eleven, then eleven-thirty. The Cadillac purred through the silent night like a giant cat at a steady forty miles an hour.

The headlight caught a white sign, Hannook River. "Pull over on the bridge up there, Pickle," Price ordered.

"But—"

"Just pull over like I say."

When the Cadillac stopped, Price put an open hand over the seat. "The gun, Pickle, give me the gun."

"I ain't going to do it, Price, we might run into the highway patrol."

"The gun, Pickle, and your hat and your jacket. Quick! We can't sit here all night arguing."

Pickle took the pistol from the seat beside him, making sure the safety was on. Next, the straw hat he bought in Crowheart and his jacket. Price wriggled out of the jacket Jethro had given him. He opened the door and went to the railing. In the half moonlight, the river below looked deep and muddy. He dropped the gun and their hats and jackets into the stream.

"I'm going to sleep now, if I can," he told the boy.

"Okay. I'll wake you up when we get to the bus station."

A little after one o'clock, another white sign told him the state line was a mile ahead. The road had been deserted for the last hour. As the Cadillac came around a curve, Pickle saw a man swinging a light in the road ahead. One highway patrol car was parked on the right, headed across the state line; another car was pulled over to the left headed toward him.

"Get down on the floor, Price, and don't move!" he shouted. "Highway patrol." In his mirror Pickle saw the distant lights of another car behind him. He slowed to a stop next to the patrolman.

"Good evening," said the patrolman, touching the brim of his hat. "Where are you bound for?"

"Florida," Pickle responded.

"All the way from California?"

"Yes, sir."

The officer glanced from the front of the Cadillac to the rear. "It's a mighty fine car. Sixteen cylinder, isn't it?"

"Yes, sir. What's wrong, sir?"

"Trouble back down the road. A young guy busted a colored boy out of jail. Armed and dangerous, they say. Could I see your license, please?"

Pickle reached in his front pocket like he was looking for his license. He heard the other patrolman shout, "There's a pickup coming."

"You can move on through," the officer told Pickle. "Be sure to stop if you get tired. Florida's a long way to go."

"Phew," Pickle let his breath out. "Did you hear all of that, Price? They're already looking for us. Good thing we ain't in the Dodge. We fooled them, didn't we, Price? You can go on back to sleep now."

At three-thirty Price drove past the bus depot. It was the only lighted place in the city. One bus, Miami printed over the windshield, was about to pull out. Another was unloading on the ramp. Pickle found a side street beyond the depot and parked. Price was still asleep. Pickle was hungry, and he felt the need to stretch his legs. I'll find out when the Detroit bus comes through, he thought, and get a hamburger and coffee.

The depot was half-filled with people, sleeping on benches, comforting babies, sitting over empty cups in the lunchroom. In the next room, patient black men in overalls and women in flowered dresses, some of them holding sleeping children, waited. Pickle went to the ticket window. Two people were ahead of him. An anxious woman was explaining where she wanted to go to the man behind the grill.

From the corner of his eye Pickle caught sight of a deputy coming in the door, his hand resting lightly on his pistol. He scanned the room, then stood at the entrance to the colored waiting room. He studied each of the men in the room. He pushed his hat back on his head and marched to the ticket window. He excused himself to the woman and spoke quietly to the agent, who shook his head. The deputy went to the depot door and leaned against the wall. He waited.

Pickle reached the ticket window. He asked for the schedule and bought a ticket. In the lunchroom he ordered two hamburgers with everything, a bag of fries, two coffees with milk and sugar, and a pack of Lucky Strikes. He carried the paper bag past the officer. The man gave him a friendly smile.

Price was awake, peeping nervously out the window. "Where have you been, Pickle? I was worried."

Pickle climbed into the backseat. "I got us some hamburgers and coffee, Price, at the depot. And some cigarettes. The bus don't leave for over an hour."

"'Doesn't leave,'" Price corrected him automatically.

"Yeah, 'doesn't leave.' I had them put everything on the hamburger. Was that right?"

"That's fine, Pickle. A lot of people waiting for the bus?"

"Yeah, folks must like to travel at night. There was a New York bus stopped on the way to Miami. I thought to myself, we had been further than that. Price and I went all the way to California and back. We done—did—what we set out to do back there in Clarence's garage."

Price chewed on his hamburger. He took a swallow of coffee. "I was thinking the same thing the other day. We done—I mean, did—what we set out to do."

"You didn't want to go at first, did you, Price?"

"I guess not. I just wanted to run home to my mother. When you get out of jail, Pickle, you're scared. Leastways, I was. I wanted someone to look after me and make sure I didn't have to go back."

"You had someone to look after you, didn't you, Price?" And, speaking more slowly, "I reckon I got someone to look after me."

They were quiet. The green second hand of the clock swept around and around and around.

Close to five o'clock, the day began to lighten. Pickle gathered up the greasy papers and cups and stuffed them in the brown bag. "We had us a time, didn't we, Price?"

"We did, Pickle. Yes, we truly did. When's the bus leaving?"

"About now," Pickle said. "I already got my ticket." He reached for Pa's kit bag. He handed Price the keys to the sixteen-cylinder Cadillac touring car.

Price took the keys without thinking, then realized what was happening. "What the hell are you doing, Pickle?"

"There's a deputy sheriff watching in the depot. He's got his hand on his gun and he takes a good look at every black man that comes in. There's a bus along soon that goes through Lutherville."

| 201 |

Price started to protest.

Pickle motioned for him to be quiet. "You drive easy out of town. You got enough gas for a hundred miles. That will take you out of the state. Find yourself a station right in the middle of a city, where they won't pay you any attention. I took forty-five dollars to pay Ma back. I don't need any more. Soon as I get my license to drive out of state I'll come up for my car." He offered Price his hand. "I'll see you someday, I reckon."

Price took the boy's hand. Whatever he was once going to say he forgot. "We had us a good time, didn't we, Pickle?"

"We sure did, Price. We goldarned sure did." The boy shut the door and headed down the street to the bus depot.